Deep Breaths

I0612507

INHALE

By Richanda Bynum

Copyright

For information contact:
Richanda Bynum
richanda.bynum.author@gmail.com

Library of Congress Control Number: 2023916505
ISBN- 13 978-1-957552-07-1
ISBN- 10 1-9575520-77-X

10 9 8 7 6 5 4 3 2 1

"All you have to do is fall, I'll catch you."

-Unknown

Chapter One

Tick tock.

Inhale, then exhale.

With the sound of my loud breathing and the ticking of the clock on the wall, one would think I was in this office all alone. However, that is not the case. Across from me sits a beautiful woman with silky mocha skin and big, beautiful brown eyes. Her eyes pierce me the same way they did when I was a child getting scolded for something. I look down at my hands, playing with my fingers, why is this so difficult? I have known this woman my whole life, this should be easy.

"Ariah, start from wherever you want. I have cancelled all my appointments for the day. So, you can just take your time," Dr. Blackwood says with eager eyes.

Michelle Anne Blackwood is what the certificate on the wall reads. She is my aunt whom I call Shelly. She is also the smartest, most caring woman I know. So, as I said, this should be easy. Where should I start?

"Look sweetie, even though this was your idea, if you would like, I can make a recommendation for you to see someone else." As usual, her soothing voice calms me.

"No, you are the only person I feel comfortable with. I cannot trust anyone else," I begin stuttering. "I want someone," I take a deep breath, "no, I need someone to know." My heart is racing, taking another deep breath I begin to tell my therapist about the trauma I have forced myself to survive.

I often wish the beginning of my life started out like everyone else's. You know how little girls start out believing they are princesses, wanting to run around the house in pretty dresses as they play with barbies? They cry, scream and throw tantrums as they please, with the excuse that they are little girls. I used to wish that my childhood memories were happy, wholesome. However, my memories are too horrific for me to pretend that my early life had light.

The earliest memory I have is of me sitting curled up in the closet of a hotel room waiting for my mother's guest to leave. I could hear my mother and the strange man grunting and cursing. Whenever my mother brought company into the room, I was sent into the closet with clear instructions to be as quiet as a mouse. I could always hear everything going on in the room though.

Sometimes my mother would be yelling and cursing, other times she would be whispering as if she were comforting a baby. One thing I knew for certain was that everyday there was a different man. Once I asked her out of curiosity, why I had to be in the closet and not make a sound.

"Because I don't trust these cock suckers, ain't no telling what they'd try to do to you for free." She grabbed my face. "The world sucks. This is a very harsh reality that you and I are living in. So always listen to what I say."

I thought my mother was everything, she would sing and play with me all day. Whenever it was my birthday, she would buy me cake, but every single night, I had to go into the closet. Most days I would fall fast asleep, but not that day, my excitement wouldn't let me. It was my birthday, the only day I would get to go outside of this small hotel room.

This was also the only day my mother would take me to eat cake.

Sitting in the closet, I was doing the best I could to keep quiet. But my 5-year-old brain could not contain all my excitement. When I saw the strange man pulling his pants up while my mother counted her money, I thought this was my chance. So, I opened the closet door.

"Mommy, can we go get cake now?" I asked, waiting for her to say yes.

"Hello there," the man said to me before looking back at my mother. "Marilynn, what's this?" The stranger started walking towards me, but my mother jumped off the bed rushing in front of him.

"Baby, how about you and I go play around a little more? Just you and me." Her hand was moving around in his pants.

"Now Marilynn, you know what I like and how I like it, so why have you been hiding such a pretty young girl in the closet?" He didn't take his eyes off me, even as my mother had her hand in his pants. The stranger pushed my mother's hand away, giving her the attention she wanted. "How much?"

My mother turned away from the both of us and took a seat in the worn out chair in the corner. Getting comfortable, she looked at me, took a cigarette out and lit it. Even though I was just a little girl, I could sense that everything around me was about to change. I always wondered how different my life would have been if I had contained myself and not opened that closet door. Maybe she would have protected me like a mother should protect their child.

"George, get the fuck out. My child is not for sale, and even if she was, you sick fuck, you wouldn't be able to afford her." Putting her cigarette out, she looked at me. "Ariah, come here."

Hesitantly, I walked out of the closet and towards my mother. The stranger's eyes tracked my movement across the room. I felt a chill run through my body, and even then, I knew that something wasn't right.

"Now Lynnie baby, I know you, just as you know me." George took a seat on the bed facing me and my mother. "I know that with you there's always a price, so stop your bullshitting and tell it to me. I'm getting a bit impatient." I looked up at my mother, concerned because this strange man was still here, and I still had not gotten my cake. My mother looked down at me as she spoke words that haunts me in my dreams to this day.

"Ariah baby, it looks like our reality was complete shit after all." She took my hand and walked me over to the strange man and introduced us, "Ariah, this is George, George, this is Ariah."

Leaning back in my chair, I tilt my head and stare at the ceiling. The ceiling art is beautiful. The intricate lines and circles are strangely comforting. Dr. Blackwood has thought of everything, I can tell she took her time when decorating her office. I feel like I can tell her anything, but maybe that's because I'm finally at my wits end. I feel like any day now, I'm due to explode. I'm tired of keeping it all in.

"Do you hate your mother?" Dr. Blackwood asks, breaking my train of thought.

"Hate?" I take a minute to think. "I don't know. I've never known how I should feel about her. I can tell you that was a pretty fucked up birthday gift." I begin laughing. "I mean, think about it, I was allowed to go outside one day out of the whole year, allowed to eat cake on one day." I could feel the tears coming. "And on that one day she sold everything innocent about me to some fat, funky, child molesting asshole named George. Hate? I don't think that word could even explain how I feel."

As usual, Dr. Blackwood has no reaction to my outburst. I have to give it to her, she is a professional. The life I lived until I met her was shit. Of course, at the time I didn't know how living that way would affect me. As Dr. Blackwood stares at me, waiting for me to speak, I have a revelation.

"You know Shelly, if my childhood didn't happen to me the way it did, I don't think I would have met you or daddy for that matt-,"she cuts me off.

"That is not an excuse, even without the traumatizing events that took place in your life, you would have met me eventually. If anything, I blame us for not coming to get you sooner." She is upset. I have been doted on and loved so much over the years by Shelly and father, that I figured I had to have that childhood so I could receive all the love I get now.

"Shelly, I'm doing the best I can to not be damaged." The tears are flowing, and snot is pouring from my nose. I feel like I'm having an emotional breakdown. I can tell she is affected by my tears, so I try to calm down, but I can't. Dr.

Blackwood begins writing notes on her pad, she stops and looks over at me.

"Ariah, what happened the day your father and I came to pick you up?" Looking up at the ceiling again, I take a deep breath.

I became a child that could not smile, and my mother became someone I feared. The closet was now a place that I sought out for peace and tranquility. I was safest there. Even during the days when there was not a stranger around, I would stay in the closet. This annoyed my mother; she had turned into someone I had never seen before. All I understood was that I did not want any of those strangers touching me. Their touch brought pain. Even when I would scream and cry, they wouldn't stop. And when they were done, they would give my mother money and leave.

Today, like any other day I sat in the closet, waiting for the stranger to leave. When someone was there, I couldn't sleep. I didn't know what would happen to me, or when I would get yanked out of the closet. As I sat there not moving a muscle, I prayed that they would both die right there on that bed. They were going at it like wild animals. The stifling odor of the room made me want to throw up. But I didn't want to leave the closet, so I suffered silently.

"Damn Luke, did your dick get longer?" my mother said, getting out of bed to light a cigarette.

"Lynnie, you know me baby, this right here been touching the floor since I came out the pussy." Luke was standing at the edge of the bed wiping himself with the bed sheets. He walked over to my mother, taking the cigarette out of her mouth, he began forcing her head towards his manhood.

My mother tried to push him away. "Look baby, I'm tired, can I take a smoke break? We've been at it for two days now."

"Bitch, I'm paying you for these services, right? My dick is still hard so bring your white ass over here and take care of it," Luke said as he began stroking himself. I could tell my mother was exhausted, she just sat there staring at the closet. Knowing what was coming next, I pushed myself deeper into the closet. Why did she have to keep doing this to me?

"Baby, what if I could offer you something different?" she asked, while taking another drag from her cigarette.

"What you mean? We been in here for 2 days, I'm sure I've seen everything you got." Luke looked confused.

"I mean, I got something over in the closet that you might be interested in, but it's gon' be $500 more."

"In the closet? Bitch, what you got in there, toys? I'm not with that. I paid to fuck you. Now get up and give me my money's worth." Luke said all this while walking towards the closet.

My heart began to beat faster and faster. Why, why did she have to be like this? My legs had begun to cramp, my stomach was growling, and I had pissed all over the floor. My mother literally left me in this closet for two whole days with no food or water. I felt tears slide down my face as the closet door swung open.

Luke opened the closet door expecting a box of sex toys, but what he saw instead was me, a little brown skinned girl with tangled curls sitting in a pee puddle, looking like she would pass out from dehydration at any moment. The only clothing I had on at the time was a dingy, too small white t-shirt and underwear. Luke looked around the closet, the place I spent most of my time. He stared at the pee and bloodstained underwear I was wearing. He turned immediately, rushing to my mother.

"Bitch, there's been a child in here this whole time, are you fucking stupid?" Luke grabbed my mother by her stringy blonde hair and threw her to the ground. "Where the fuck you steal this child from, huh, bitch?"

My mother laid on the floor with fear in her eyes. "Steal? I didn't steal her, that's my daughter Luke, calm down baby. I'm tired; she'll finish you off."

Luke slaps her the proceeds to punch her three times. As she lays on the dirty carpeted floor, he catches his breath then kicks her.

"Hoe, are you insane? Your own daughter, bitch? The fuck is wrong with you? That's a little fucking girl." Luke turned to look at me, then back at my mother. "Finish me off, how? Bitch, that is a fucking child." He kicked my mother in her rib cage, she cried out begging him to stop, but just like mine, her cries went unheard.

Luke couldn't control himself as he continued to hit my mother. Later, I learned that something similar had happened to his older sister as a child. He had been a child himself at the time, so he couldn't do anything to protect her from his drug addicted mother and her drug dealers. The trauma that his mother forced on his sister changed her and when she turned sixteen, she took her own life. As he hit my mother, he saw her as his own.

Still pissed and tired, he left my mother on the dirty floor sobbing and walked over to me.

"Hey little princess, you want to go with me? I'll get you cleaned up and fed." I looked over to my mother, her once white skin now covered in purple and blue. Blood was dripping from her mouth as she reached her hand out, whispering in her soft, alluring voice that I should go to her.

"Shut the fuck up. Your chance to be a mother is gone," Luke yelled. He turned back to me, he was not standing too close, he saw how afraid I was. "Nothing bad will happen to you, okay, look." He grabbed his underwear and pants, slid them on, then took his police badge out of his pocket. "I'm a cop, I'll take you to get cleaned up and get some food." Luke held his hand out towards me.

"Fuck you Luke, you ain't taking my baby! That is my child, and I can do whatever I please with her." My mother managed to pick herself up off the floor. She sat in her chair and lit her cigarette.

"Where's her father?" Luke asked, while still looking at me with his hand out.

"Father? That motherfucker don't even know she exist." Getting comfortable she crossed her legs. "Shit, he somewhere living lavish with his wife. How the fuck should I know?"

"Do you know who he is?" Luke turned to look at my mother.

"Yeah, I know that nigga," my mother answered. Luke looked at my mother as if he wanted to hit her again.

"What's his name?"

"Why? So you can take her down to the station and get in contact with him. That motherfucker ain't gon' show up." My mother threw her head back while laughing. This was the first time I had heard her say anything about my father. "How about this Luke the savior, take her, go see if he cares. But, if he does not claim her, I'm coming for my child. She won't be in the system." With a confused look on his face, Luke looked at me again. His eyes scanned my small, frail body then drifted back to the closet I had been cooped up in for the past two days.

"What's his name? I'm not gon' ask your stupid ass again," Luke said through clenched teeth. Luke inhaled deeply. *"At least in the system she could have a childhood."* Instead of waiting for me to come to him, he picked me up. My mother stood as he walked me to the door.

"Charles Blackwood." She took a long drag from her cigarette. *"Fuck the system Luke, where you think my childhood went?"*

"Was your mother also abused as a child?" Dr. Blackwood asks while looking at me.

"I never got the chance to ask her. The day Officer Luke took me was the last time I saw her face."

"What happened after that?" Dr. Blackwood asks, as she starts writing in her pad again. I look at the painting she has on the wall behind her, and I get lost in its colors.

When we got to the hospital, a nurse Luke knew rushed over and took me out of his arms.

"Luke, what the fuck? Where did you find this child?" she asked rushing down a hall.

"In a hotel closet. Take care of her for me, make sure she's okay. But from what she's been through, I'm sure that's not going to be the case. Feed her and I'll bring her some

clothes, I gotta go contact her father." Luke walked over to me. "Ariah, this nice, pretty nurse is going to take care of you for a minute, I'll be right back." I grabbed his arm; I didn't know this lady and I hated strangers. Luke looked at me, smiling softly. "I promise you, no one is going to hurt you here." I let go of his hand and he left.

Lots of people came in and out of my room. All of them were women. Every time someone came in, their eyes looked as if they had just been crying. After I was examined, everyone came to know the horror I had been put through. I remained silent, watching as they tiptoed around me with their forced smiles.

Officer Luke came back with clothes, like he said he would. As he entered the room, a tall, beautiful lady with chocolate colored skin walked in behind him. She walked over to me and hugged me as tightly as she could, causing my breath to momentarily get stuck in my chest. My pent up emotions hit me all at once and the tears just started flowing. I wasn't sure if it was her, or if it was the fact that I had just needed to be hugged. The door opened again and a tall, brown skinned man that resembled the beautiful lady walked in. The man looked at me as I looked at him. The beautiful lady stood up off the bed and went over to him, and they both stared at me.

"Charles, there is no denying it. This child is ours," the beautiful lady whispered. Her smile was so wide that it looked like her eyes were closed. "Even if you wanted to, you couldn't, we'll be taking her with us." She walked back over to me, gently grabbing my hand, she placed her palm against my face. "Don't worry, Ariah. We're here and I'm so sorry it took us so long. My name is Michelle and I'm your aunt."

"And I," the man walked closer to the bed getting a better look at my face, "am your father, Charles Blackwood."

My aunt Michelle pushed my father away and looked at me. "Is there anything I can get you? Are you hungry? Have you eaten?"

I don't remember the last time I had spoken. It might have been weeks, months or that whole year. But at that moment, there was only thing I could think to say.

"I want cake, it's my birthday."

Dr. Blackwood listens to me intently. Though this was my idea, I am still extremely nervous. I don't know how she will look at me from now on. When I was a child, no one asked me about what happened when I lived with my mother. I thought everyone wanted me to forget, now I realize that they've just been waiting for me to tell them myself. Asking Shelly to be my therapist was my way of doing that.

"Can we stop here for today?" I ask, my mouth widens in an unexpected yawn and I suddenly realize how tired I am.

"Of course," Dr. Blackwood says as she closes her notebook and stops the timer.

When the timer is on, she's Dr. Michelle Blackwood, but once the timer is off, she is my beautiful aunt Shelly. I stand, grabbing my things, Shelly rushes over to me and hugs me tightly, just like she did that day at the hospital.

"I love you Shelly," I say smiling. I take comfort in her hugs. She pulls away, staring at me, then turns and walks back over to her desk.

"When would you like to come in for your next appointment?" Dr. Blackwood asks, reverting to professional mode.

"Any Tuesday that you have an opening should be okay."

"I'll clear all my Tuesdays and dedicate them just to you."

"You don't have to do tha-", she cuts me off.

"Yes, I do. Remember, it always has and always will be-."

"Us over everything," I interject.

Walking out of the office, I feel refreshed and relieved. Today marks a new day. I decide to walk home. I love walking because it gives me a chance to think and get my thoughts in order. I replay the session in my mind, I remember everything that happened to me. I even remember what the horrid room smelled like. It was like leaving a tangerine in your backpack over summer break. The sour, rotten odor of that room will stay with me for as long as I live. I shake my head in disgust.

Making it to my lavish apartment building, I nod at the doorman as I enter. I stop at my mailbox knowing it's empty, then I walk over to the elevator. The doors open, revealing a couple inside, I step to the side allowing them to walk by. Even to this day, I don't like being touched. Entering my apartment, I throw my things on the floor diving into my plush couch. I place my face into the cushion to muffle my scream. Finally, I did it. I finally told Shelly what happened. I roll over getting comfortable, this space is the only place I can actually breathe. I have everything I need right here. My phone begins to vibrate, I pick it up and see a text from my boyfriend, Chase.

Chapter Two

Crawling off the couch, I toss my phone into my purse. I dread going back outside. My phone chimes and I glance at the text Chase sent me. I groan in annoyance because now I must get up, since he plans to swing by to get me in an hour. Chase is perfect. He's kind, smart and handsome; he treats me as if I am the only girl in the world. He's the type of guy all teenage girls dream of; light hazel eyes that makes you feel like you're looking into another dimension, beautiful broad shoulders, so broad that when he hugs me, I feel like I'm being swallowed whole and a killer smile that you could never say no to. Chase is the epitome of perfection.

He was the very first boy I talked to when I arrived here for college. Being from the east coast, I didn't know anyone except my aunt and no one knew me. I literally used college as a way for me to get away. I thought this place was a safe haven, where I could start fresh and not need or know anybody; Chase had other plans. For the first 4 months I ignored him, treated him horribly, but he didn't back down. He kept coming at me like there was no tomorrow, and I became intrigued. All it took was one smile and I was a goner; I remember the day clearly.

My fridge was empty, so I got my lazy butt up and went to the grocery store. Making my way through the store, I stopped in my tracks. There Chase stood in the refrigerator aisle looking at the expiration date on a half-gallon bottle of milk. Usually, I would ignore him and continue my shopping, but that day I was feeling friendly.

"Hey milkmaid," I said giggling to myself, remembering the line from "Clerks", one of my favorite movies.

"Ariah," he said, with a look of surprise.

"Am I interrupting you? You looked so serious, that I couldn't just walk by without saying something," I said feeling awkward.

"No, no, I'm just mesmerized by how beautiful you are, this the first time I've seen you smile. I'm amazed." His comment made me blush and I realized that he had always been like this with me. His way with words bothered me

because they made me think of someone else. Someone I didn't want to think about, someone that I had run away from. "Ariah, did I offend you? I really like you, but every time I tell you what I'm thinking, it's like you put this wall up." His words sounded sincere, which left me with a heavy feeling of guilt in the pit of my stomach.

"If I were ugly, would you be this interested in me? Instead of focusing on my face, what about how I think, what I feel, who I am? I don't want feelings from anyone based on how beautiful I am." I knew he didn't deserve this, but why should I worry about how he felt? I was tired of moving to the beat of someone else's drum. I got upset and started to walk away, I was hungry and wanted to continue my shopping so I could go home. Chase ran in front of me with his hands up in the air.

"Ariah," I started to walk around him. "Wait, please." I stopped, giving him my best death glare. "I want to get to know how you feel, what you think and who you really are. But how am I supposed to do that when you won't let me in? Yes, your looks are what made me start chasing after you, then it became about me trying to get you to open up." He paused as if he was trying to find the right words. "When I *call you beautiful, that's what I think at that moment; when I say, 'I like you', that's what I feel. I can't help but say the things I think and feel when I think and feel them, because that's who I am." Chase looked totally defeated. "I can't promise you that I'll leave you alone, because I feel like I could chase after you forever," he chuckled then looked me straight in my eyes. "My name is Chase after all."*

I couldn't help it, right there in the milk aisle of my neighborhood grocery store, I fell over in laughter. It felt so good. I hadn't laughed so hard in such a long time. How could he be so cheesy? How could he be so perfect? He hadn't realized that just walking up and talking to him on my own, was me opening up. I had gotten used to him randomly coming up to me saying anything he was thinking. In that moment, I thought, he must really like me. People were looking at us like we were crazy because we were laughing so loud and hard, but it didn't matter. Nothing mattered, it felt like it was just me and him.

After that encounter, we started dating. How could I not accept him? His sincerity moved me. Chase introduced me to his frat, which by the way, I did not know he was a part of. I didn't know a lot about Chase, but I was willing to learn and that made him happy. We've been dating for a year and a half. I am now in my junior year of college. Everything is perfect, we are perfect. I haven't told Chase about my childhood, and I don't plan to. Only two people know my story and for now, I want to keep it that way.

Our relationship is PG-13 at best. I have intimacy issues; I don't like being touched. Chase understands this, so we take things at my pace. It took us a year to kiss, but taking things slow is the best I can do. I cringe when he kisses me, but I don't run. I want him to know that I'm trying. I'm pretty sure he's aware that something has traumatized me, but he never asks. Chase never pressures me into anything, he always makes me feel safe. Like I said before, the epitome of perfection.

Now showered and changed, I collapse on my couch waiting for him to knock on my door. His frat is throwing a party and he wants me to be there. Chase always wants to walk around with me on his arm as if I am a trophy. At first, I was like no, hell no, but then I started getting used to it. In high school, I was the center of everyone's attention, no matter how hard I tried not to be. So being so in college was inevitable. Chase is friendly, he doesn't judge anyone, he welcomes all, in turn everyone loves him. Did I mention gorgeous? Whenever I go anywhere with him I get glares, which I am also used to.

A knock at the door causes me to jump. I know it's Chase, he's the only person who ever knocks on my door. I grab my bag and head to the door. As soon as I open it, Chase pulls me to him, engulfing me in his warm embrace.

"Oh, how I have missed you. You smell perfect as always." Feeling a bit uncomfortable, I pull away and he reluctantly releases me.

"Well, are we going to stand here all night or are you going to take me to this party you've been blowing me off for all week?" I pout playfully. I love acting spoiled around him. Chase takes my hand and we walk out the apartment. He looks at our intertwined hands and smiles. We get down to his car and he opens the door for me. Much like mine, Chase's parents are well off. His father is a movie producer and his mother a screenwriter. We don't talk about our parents much, him not wanting to live in their shadow and me not wanting to scare him off. Chase doesn't know who my father is; just that he is an entrepreneur. This is something else that I like about him, he never pries and neither do I, we just go with the flow. Looking out the window of his Camaro, I feel his hand grab mine.

"Ariah, I told my mother about us." I turn to face him, giving him my full attention. "She keeps bugging me about meeting some girl, so I told her about you and how I feel about you." He stops talking, I guess he's waiting for my response.

"And?" I say, staring at him. I'm sure there is more.

"Well, she wants to meet you. She asked if we could come up this weekend for dinner." His eyes are on the road, "before you get upset, I still haven't given her an answer. I wanted to talk to you first."

"I don't know," I respond nervously. "I mean, do your parents know that I'm black?"

Chase takes his hand away from mine. "What the hell Ariah, why does that matter?" I can see his jaw clenching. "Should I have said, oh yeah, mom hold back your racism, Ariah is black." I stare at him as his face turns a bright, tomato red. "My parents aren't like that. I'm not like that." He is clearly angry, which in turn causes me to become annoyed.

"Don't sit there and make it seem like I'm wrong for asking. You never talk about them, so I thought--." He cuts me off.

"That I'm hiding my racist parents from my black girlfriend?"

"Look, whether you like it or not, it's a thing, and you shouldn't be offended by my asking." The silence in the vehicle is suffocating. We've never talked about this before, we never had to. I wish I could say I don't see color, but that is not even remotely the case. I've been through this kind of thing before. It doesn't matter who my father is or that I am half white, my skin is brown and that's what I'm judged by. He glances at me and I don't try to hide the anger that bubbles up inside me.

"I'm sorry I got defensive," he sighs softly. "My parents aren't like that and they didn't raise me to be like that." Chase grabs my hand, I let him, and it's evident that I'm slowly caving.

"No, I'm sorry. I've been through something like this before. I just don't want to be disappointed." We pull into a parking spot. All around us, dozens of people are heading in the direction of his frat house. Chase pulls my hand up to his lips and gently kisses my palm.

"You won't be disappointed, now let's go let loose and have some fun." He gets out the car, walks to my side and graciously opens the door.

"I don't know about loose, but I can do fun," I say, laughing as I exit the car. With Chase holding my hand tightly, we walk up to the house. You can most definitely tell there is a party going on here. The frat throws this party every year to celebrate the new brothers that are joining. We can't even make it up the walkway without someone stopping Chase to talk. Yet another thing I've gotten use to, Chase's popularity. Chase doesn't let go of my hand as he talks to his friends, which makes me smile because I'm not going anywhere without him, he has nothing to worry about.

While standing next to Chase my eyes begin scanning everything. I smile to myself, realizing that for the first time in my life I feel normal. Here I am, a regular college student getting ready to go to a college frat party with my dreamy college boyfriend. This feels surreal. Everything feels perfect, but I already know there is no such thing as perfect, *'perfection is just a delusion'*, my father always says.

The front door of the house opens. I'm unable to see the face of the person that just walked out because of the glare from the porch light. The person begins making their way towards us. Something about their silhouette is familiar. I know that walk and as he gets closer, I realize that more than anything, I know those fucking eyes. My body stiffens and my breathing slows significantly. The closer he gets, the faster my heart starts to beat. It's as if I'm that sixteen-year-old girl again. Chase feels my hand tighten around his and looks at me with concern. Before he can voice his question, my nightmare speaks.

"Chase, my man! What's going on?" he asks, looking at Chase and completely ignoring me. "This fucking party, bro!" They slap hands together as if they've known each other since childhood.

"I know man, what did I tell you when I recruited you? This is how we fucking live, and now you do as well." Chase is so excited that he lets my hand go. He begins shouting the frat's chant. I don't know how everyone hears him, but the whole house starts chanting with him. You would think we were at a football game or something. I smile, rolling my eyes, almost forgetting who's standing in front of me.

"Oh, shit babe, my bad. Let me introduce you. Ariah, this is Samuel Conrad. Samuel, this is Ariah Blackwood, my beautiful girlfriend." Chase grabs me by the waist, pulls me close and kisses me. I kiss him back, but too soon I awkwardly pull away.

"She is everything you said she was," Samuel says smirking. I've always hated that smirk. I know he's about to start a game involving me and Chase, but I'm not going to let it happen.

"Babe, actually I know him. We went to high school together." Now, I'm the one smirking. There's no point in hiding this from Chase, Samuel will not ruin this for me.

"Really? Small world. Samuel, now you can give me the many details on how she was in high school. Did she date anybody?" My body stills when he asks this, Chase is laughing, but this line of questioning is a landmine.

"I have many stories." As Samuel speaks, his eyes never leave mine. He is telling the truth. He does in fact, know everything about me, everything.

"I have to go to the restroom. I'll be right back," I say, trying to prevent myself from panicking. I walk away without hearing Chase's response. I'm practically running towards the house. Ignoring all the curious gazes, I glance around in search of an empty room. My throat feels as if it's slowly sealing shut and I realize that I'm hyperventilating. Thankfully, I find an empty room and I quickly close the door behind me shutting out the sounds of chatter and music.

"Deep breaths, deep breaths. You are fine Ariah, you are fine." Shit, this pep talk is not working. I begin pacing the bedroom floor, the door opens, then closes quickly. There he stands, before I can say anything or protest, he hugs me tight.

"Shh, take a deep breath. You're safe. I'm here." My breathing begins to calm. This is all it takes. I just need to be in his arms, and I'll be calm. Inhaling his scent almost makes me dizzy with joy, I could stay right here forever, but I'm not that girl anymore. I don't want to be, and for the first time since we met, I push him away. We stand staring at each other. I know he has questions, but I don't want to answer them.

I try to walk past him, but he stops me, grabs my arms and pushes me up against the wall. My heart is pounding painfully, which it always does when he's around. I want to move, but my legs won't comply. My eyes begin to water as they stare into his beautiful blue ones. It's been a long time since I've seen them, but I still quiver at the sight of them. I know what this means and Samuel does too. His face drifts closer to mine. I know what I have to say to stop him, but the words won't come.

"I have Chase," I whisper instead.

"Tsk, tsk, tsk," he says, his face still dangerously close to mine. "You know those are not the magic words. Ariah, stop me if you want, you know how. Or have you forgotten?" He places his hand on my cheek, wiping away the single tear that has managed to escape. I can't handle this situation, this intensity; my emotions are running wild.

"Do I need to remind your body who I am?" His hand moves down my face, his thumb now caressing my bottom lip. My eyes watch his, as his eyes follow the movement of his fingers against my lips. Samuel is about to move in for a kiss when a loud knock echoes through the room.

"Is anybody using this room? We are trying to fuck." The muffled voice behind the door isn't one I recognize. I close my eyes and exhale in relief. Saved by some drunken idiot. I push Samuel off me and rush out the door. I'm so disgusted with myself. I must be the dumbest bitch on the planet. How could I still feel something for him? How could my body betray me again like it did in the past? Why didn't I just tell him I don't want him? That's all I had to say. The truth leaves a bitter taste in my mouth. Samuel still has me in the palm of his hands. I am still trapped in his endless mind games. I thought I had escaped, but I've been fooling myself.

I search the house looking for Chase, I find him standing next to his friends and some girl I don't know. I've never seen her before, and I don't like the way she has her hand resting comfortably on Chase's shoulder. I paste a smile on my face and walk up to them.

"Hey what's up everybody?" Chase immediately grabs my arm pulling me to him.

"Where have you been? I was looking for you," he says, kissing my cheek.

"Well, not hard enough." I'm staring directly at the girl as I speak. What the fuck is wrong with me? I was about to be kissed by someone else just moments ago, but I'm so fucked up that none of that matters. Chase is fucking mine. Chase picks up on what I'm getting at, he turns my face so that I'm looking at him.

"Baby, all I see is you, nobody else." I smile, because I believe he's telling the truth. I'm just feeling guilty about what I almost let happen upstairs. Chase is who I want, he is who I want to love.

As Chase and I stand in the corner cuddled against each other, I feel eyes watching at me. I don't look in their direction because I already know who they belong to. I have gotten so use to being looked at intensely by those eyes, I can always feel when they're on me. I want to go home, but I know how important this night is to Chase. I'll just have to suck it up and be stared at all night. One thing is for sure, I'm not leaving his side. I'm with Chase and this is where I want to be.

Walking into my apartment, I throw everything on the floor, including my clothes and head to bed. I put my phone on the charger and briefly glance at the time. I'm grateful I don't have classes today since it's seven in the morning. The party was literally all night. I need to speak to Shelly as soon as possible because my mind is in a frenzy. I send her a text asking if I can come in sometime today. Fuck next week, too much is happening, and I need to talk to her now. Immediately after sending the text, I fall asleep.

I wake up to seven missed calls and two texts. Two of the calls are from Chase, one is from daddy and four are from an unknown number. I know who the unknown number is; he is still crazy as hell. I ignore daddy because I know what he wants to talk about. My father only cares about one thing these days. Shelly sent me a text letting me know I can come in today at four. Looking at the time, I still have plenty of time to get ready. I sigh, looking down at my phone. Should I open his messages? Do I want to know what he has to say?

"I know you know it's me. Stop being like this, I miss you. I need to see you." I stare numbly at the text, reading it repeatedly. Why did he find me? Shit, how did he find me? I

need to get my shit together. Deleting the messages, I dial Chase's number.

"Hey beautiful, just waking up?" Chase asks. I smile at the sound of his voice.

"Yes, I'm about to head out in a bit. I just wanted to hear your voice. What are you doing?" I hear noise in his background. "What's all that noise in the background?"

"Me and the boys about to play footba-", his voice cuts off.

"Hey beautiful, you don't have to worry. We won't hurt your boyfriend." I know this voice; a shiver shoots up my spine. I can hear Chase yelling at Samuel for calling me beautiful.

"Give me my phone back, asshole." I stare at my wall in confusion. How have the two of them become this close without me even knowing? When did they become friends? How long has Chase known Samuel? "Hey babe, I love you. I'll call you later." I try to say something, but the phone goes dead.

I don't know how I should act. It feels like my perfect world is crumbling. I get up, shower and get dressed. I stare at myself in the mirror for a moment, I'm starting to hate my reflection all over again. *"I like Chase, I like Chase. I want to be with Chase"*, I tell myself this repeatedly. I will not give in, not again. I grab my things and walk out of my apartment.

Chapter Three

"You're back early," Dr. Blackwood says while searching for my file.

"A lot has happened since I last spoke to you. After yesterday, I realize it's better to let it all go instead of holding on to it." I'm not as nervous as I was yesterday.

"Alright, where do you want to start? I'm listening and ready whenever you are." With pen in hand and note pad on her lap, Dr. Blackwood looks at me. I lay back so I can look up at the ceiling as I talk.

"Let's go back to when everything changed for me. When my life became even more complicated than it already was."

By now, I had settled into my new life. The day after I was discharged from the hospital, my father and aunt moved me from Atlanta to Connecticut. It was the first time I had traveled anywhere. Everything around me was new and shiny, but I couldn't enjoy them. My seven-year-old eyes had become tainted. I saw the world and people differently. I didn't trust anyone but Officer Luke and now my Aunt Shelly. I held her hand tightly, not letting go once we left the hospital. Maybe my young mind thought she looked too much like a princess to be evil.

My father, who introduced himself as Charles Blackwood, didn't take his eyes off me even once. I was still trying to figure out if I could trust him or not. When we arrived at our destination, there were two black fancy looking sedans with giant men in suits. I tightened my hold on Shelly's hand, she looked down at me and smiled.

"Don't worry, these men will protect you, nothing bad will ever happen to you again. Every one of them knows how important you are to your father and me. They will protect you with their lives." Shelly kneeled and caressed my cheek, a bright smile lit up her face. I didn't say anything, I believed her, so I followed her. We got into the car, and I sat in the middle. I don't remember how long the car ride was, but when we drove through some huge golden gates, I gasped. It looked like a castle, but way bigger than the ones I saw in the princess books my mother once read to me. My father saw the look on my face.

"This is our home," he said as we got out the car. Still not saying a word, I looked around. My father grabbed my hand gently.

"You are a Blackwood, all of this is yours." We made our way up the grand stairs and into the house. "Now that I have you, the world will deny you nothing." My father walked me to a couch and sat me down next to him. I was shaking, but I didn't move.

"The life you lived before coming here, the pain you felt, forget all about that. I will give you everything and kill all those who try to harm you." I watched as his eyes began to water. "I can't change what happened to you, but we will rewrite it." He got up and walked out the room. Shelly ran over to me and hugged me, and maybe I was getting used to her hugs because I didn't feel like pushing her away.

"Your daddy is not good at showing his emotions. When he found out about you, I thought he'd kill your mother for keeping you from him." She paused, a pained look creased her face. "Especially when he talked to your doctor." Shelly closed her eyes and sighed. "But all that is behind us, behind you. If you ever need anything, never hesitate to speak. Your voice will get you anything you want." She wiped away her tears. "Now come on, let's get you cleaned up, I want to show you your room."

The day I arrived at the Blackwood mansion was the first and only time I ever saw my father cry. My father has never shown any weaknesses, he is proud and arrogant. He is the first in his family to acquire wealth. He grew up poor and had nothing. His whole life, he worked with one goal in mind, his legacy. He told me he hated his parents for leaving him and his little sister with nothing, not even a pot to piss in. My father fought to be the best in school while hustling to feed himself and his sister. He got a scholarship to college and never looked back.

Charles Blackwood is now one of the most successful black men in the world. His business consists of subsidizing other businesses. How nice of him to help those in need, right? Wrong. He's more like a loan shark. If he helps you, he wants to be paid back in full or he will take your company apart and sell it piece by piece. My father is ruthless and cold. He doesn't have time to beat around the bush, when it comes to business, he's straightforward and menacing. Well, that's how the world sees him. I admire my father, everything he says to me I take it in. For the past eight years, he has been laying the *groundwork for me to become his heir. He doesn't care that I'm a girl, the only thing that matters is that I am a Blackwood.*

When I first arrived, I didn't speak for 3 months. At first, this drove him crazy, but Shelly calmed him, telling him I needed time. Taking her advice, he relaxed and became more patient. The first time I spoke in the mansion was to my father. He was standing at the dining room window in the middle of a call.

"Look John, fuck you, fuck Claire and fuck Joon. You think I give a fuck about Clay's sob story? Why are you all being lenient? Tell that mothafucker not to make me fly down there." He hung up, turned from the window and noticed me.

I guess he hadn't seen me when I walked in and took a seat at the table. There were rules that had to be followed in the Blackwood mansion. We always ate dinner together, no matter what. My father would make sure he was at home by seven every day. Shelly said he was a softy and just wanted to have a reason to see us every day. I liked this rule, I hated eating alone because I didn't want to be left alone with my thoughts.

This particular day Shelly hadn't gotten to the table yet. She must have still been studying, so it was just me and my father sitting at the table. Though I didn't speak, my father would still talk to me and wait for my answer. Today was no different, I stared at him, as Shelly entered the room.

"Sorry I'm late, I don't know why I thought getting my Ph.D. would be easy." She took a seat across from me.

"The things you want in life will never be easy, that's why you have to work hard. Easy things aren't worth it," my father said looking at me. "Ariah," the maids walked in, quietly placing our food in front of us. He waited until they were gone to speak. "What do you want to be when you grow up?" I was seven and damaged, and I'd never thought about it. What did I want to be when I grew up? I knew I didn't want to be weak. I wanted to be able to protect myself and those I loved. I didn't want my body to be sold. I didn't want to be betrayed by someone I loved, I wanted to be strong. We sat there looking into each other eyes. I felt my eyes watering, I wanted to say it, I wanted my voice to be heard. Shelly's words echoed in my head, 'your voice will get you anything', so I made my decision and opened my mouth.

"I want to be like you." Tears fell from my eyes, but I didn't make a sound. I had been quiet for three months. This man had saved and protected me. He was the strongest person I knew. He was who I wanted to be when I grew up. My father sat there looking at me, his hand touched my face as he wiped my tears away. We were all silent for a minute, taking in the moment. Realizing that I was truly safe, my emotions erupted.

"Like me, huh?" he cut into his steak. "Well, it's going to be hard work, and you can't change your mind later." He ate a piece of his meat while looking at me curiously. "Don't come crying to me later saying 'how could you take the words of a seven-year-old seriously'." I sat and listened. "We'll start tomorrow. I gotta call John and tell him what his goddaughter just said." He stood up and left the dining room.

My aunt burst out laughing and I stared at her in confusion. "Good luck, it's been a long time since I've seen him so happy." After saying my first words to my father, everything changed. Everyday tutors and etiquette teachers came to the house. I was always learning something from someone, my father said he didn't want me wasting my time on nonsense like toys and television. That was fine with me. I hadn't owned those things before, so they weren't missed. I was the perfect student. I didn't know much to begin with, so I was willing to learn everything. I was home schooled for eight years.

The year I turned fifteen, Shelly came up with an idea. She ran into my father's office, scaring me half to death. I was sitting on the floor looking over some files for him. He always wanted my opinion on his business plans. He was always testing me to see what I had learned and how I would handle complex scenarios.

I loved sitting in my corner of his office reading over his files. I loved watching as he conducted business from home. Sometimes, I would bring a book with me if he didn't need me to look over anything. The truth is, I loved being around him.

"Charlie, how about we enroll Ariah into high school?" I held my breath, waiting to hear my father's response.

"Seriously Shells, what did I say about bringing work home with you? Stop comparing your nut job patients to my child." My father was clearly annoyed. Whenever she had a patient that reminded her of me, she would come home with a plan to fix me.

"First of all, she's not a child, she's fifteen now, how about you loosen up a bit?" Shelly looked at me as if she wanted me to speak.

"No, everything she needs to know she can learn from me, or her tutors. I am not sending her to some school so they can undo all the work I have done. High school? Hell no." He was serious, usually Shelly would back down, but today she didn't.

"Okay, fine. But tell me, how is she supposed to conduct business correctly if she doesn't even know how to interact with people? Ariah barely leaves this house. You and I both know she is scared to. That is not normal. She needs human relationships. It is a big world out there, far more than just this mansion and she has never seen it. Keeping her locked in here will only harm her. She needs to see what the snakes look like in order to defeat them." She causally took a seat on the couch as she waited patiently for his response.

"Ariah, I won't be here to make decisions for you all your life. What do you want to do?" My father always did this. This must be another damn test. He wanted to see how I would answer, whether I would be decisive or not. High school? Sure, I was curious, but more than anything, Shelly

was right. I barely left the house; it was not because I was scared to go outside, I just didn't trust people. I did love to challenge myself, so I guess I could try it.

"Sure, I'll go, it's just another hurdle I need to get over." I looked my father dead in the eye, making sure my voice was strong and steady. "Besides, I'm not scared to go outside, I just don't like people." My father laughed.

"Fine, I'll find you a high school." He went back to his work and I sat back down to finish reading the file. I heard Shelly sigh.

"Seriously, why are you not excited? This is high school, hot guys and bitchy girls. It's what being a teenager is all about." I looked at her, sure I was excited, maybe, I think. But right now, I wanted to focus on the file. I finally saw what he wanted me to find. Someone was trying to embezzle funds. Shelly took a seat waiting for me to finish reading. When I was done, I stood up and walked over to my father ready to tell him my findings. Before I could make it across the room, Shelly jumped up, took the file out my hand, and threw it on my father's desk. Grabbing my hand, she dragged me out of the office, smiling like a crazy person.

"We're going school shopping; you'll make high school your bitch." We both laughed at how corny she was being. I grabbed a jacket and we got into her car with our bodyguards in tow. Another rule of the Blackwood mansion, if you're going outside, it does not matter where or for how long, you must never be alone. We Blackwood's always had shadows. Shopping with Shelly was so exhausting, I felt like I had been running laps for 3 hours. We got back home and all I wanted to do was sleep, but my father had other plans.

"Welcome back, perfect timing. I thought I was going to have to come get you two," he said putting his coat on.

"Are you leaving before dinner?" Shelly asked.

"No, we're having dinner with the Conrad's. I told John about Ariah going to high school, he suggested she go to the school his son goes to. Then somehow we got around to food and now we're invited to his new house for dinner." He turned us both around to walk right back out the door.

"Daddy, I'm tired," I groaned.

"I'm sure you are, but your godfather wants to see you. It's been months since you last saw him." We got into the truck.

"Oh, hush Charlie. You just want to see him. What's wrong? Did he forget he owes you money or something? I'm not breaking up any fights, not tonight, and the food better be fucking good," Shelly said with attitude as she looked out the window.

My father ignored her, it seemed like he was in a good mood and that made me smile. The Conrad house was 30 minutes away from our house. The first time I met John Conrad, my godfather, I was eight. My father was preparing to take me on a dinner date which was interrupted when John called. We ended up having to go to his office. John was tall, with blue eyes and sandy brown hair. For some reason, he reminded me of my mother.

John and my father had been friends in high school, and he was the only one my dad trusted. He's the CEO of an accounting firm, so he handles a lot of my father's accounts. I once asked my father why he trusted him not to steal.

"I know all that mothafucker's hiding spots," he had said. I laughed at that memory as we pulled into the driveway of the beautiful mansion.

This house was not as big as the Blackwood mansion, but it was not too far off. I was here to meet John's son, whom

I'd never met before. My father helped me out the truck then he helped Shelly. The front door swung open and out stepped John. My father moved toward him, calm and silent as a cheetah, and punched him right in the stomach. John doubled over, loud choking gasps escaped him.

"Fuck! You bastard! It was just $100,000, was that necessary?" Regaining his composure, John looked over at Shelly.

"The goddess is here," he says as he hugs her. "Shells, just marry me, let's make babies." John lets her go and my dad sends another swift punch to his stomach. "Goddammit, fuck!"

"You should have just given me my money. You know what's funny? I didn't catch it. Ariah was looking over the books and found the money missing." My father's face shone with pride as he looked at me. I stood there watching their interaction in awe, Shelly, of course, seemed undisturbed.

"Why do two grown men play these kinds of game with each other? Stop stealing from each other." She shook her head in annoyance.

"This is how we stay ahead, plus it keeps us from getting sloppy." My father turned to John, "now invite us in asshole. Say hi to your goddaughter."

With a pained expression, John held his hand up and waved, "hi goddaughter." I smiled and followed as he walked us in.

"So, I really can't have Shelly then?" John asked seriously. I burst into loud, uncontrollable laughter. I'd been worried he would've been angry that I had caught him stealing and not my father. But the whole time, he'd been thinking about Shelly and how my father rejected him. These were the people who were raising me. Looking around the house, I can't help thinking how beautiful it is. The ceilings are high with ornate designs and the windows are wide and elegant. John and my father are having a conversation that I can't quite hear, and Shelly is engrossed in a discussion with the maid.

Deciding to get away from them, I walked around to explore. Like my father, it would seem John is also an art collector. I hear footsteps behind me, so I turn in the direction of the approaching person and my eyes find his. I remember taking in air and holding it. I remember everything around me coming to a standstill. I couldn't take my eyes off his. With a confident smile, he held his hand out for me to take. The moment I placed my hand in his, a swarm of butterflies erupted in my stomach. My heart was pounding so loudly, I was sure he heard it. 'Deep breaths Ariah', I repeated this in my head.

"You must be Ariah, I'm Samuel."

Chapter Four

"Was it love at first sight?" Dr. Blackwood asks, forcing me out my trance.

"Love?" I pause, trying to find the answer. "I'm not sure. It was something that had never happened to me before. I remember us staring at each other that whole night. It was like the world only had me and him in it. I don't think I looked down at my food. I don't even remember what we were served." I sit up on the couch. "I don't know what came over me. But, if I knew then what I do now, I would have ignored it."

"You say you don't think it was love, but the way you just explained the two of you meeting, one would think otherwise," Dr. Blackwood says, jotting notes in her notebook.

"How did I explain it?" I ask curiously.

"Maybe not so much how you explained it, but the way you looked as you explained it. You had stars in your eyes, like you were in love with Samuel." I shift nervously in my seat. In love? Not with the bastard I swore to hate. Not some asshole who broke my heart! I ran away from my father just to get away from him. How could I be in love with him? Why did he have to find me? I was finally getting my life together. Things had finally started to feel normal again. I'm worried I might have a relapse.

"What do you mean by relapse?" Dr. Blackwood asks, pulling me out of my thoughts. Shit. Did I say that out loud? I take a deep breath.

"Samuel Conrad is an intoxicating drug to me," I put my head in my hands. "No matter when or where, the moment our eyes meet, I'm captivated, stuck and unable to move." I lay my head back on the couch looking up at the ceiling. "My heart beats so fast and so hard, I feel shivers and my body tremble uncontrollably. I wish I were exaggerating. I wish this shit was just some fucked up lie. He touches me and my whole body lights up like a flame. Samuel Conrad is an addiction that I'm running from."

For the first time, Shelly doesn't hide her shock. I smile because she's usually so skilled at keeping a neutral expression. My relationship with Samuel had been a well-guarded secret. We had never taken the time to clarify what we meant to each other. He had just pulled me along and I'd followed, holding on for dear life. To our parents, we were just god-siblings. Dr. Blackwood, finally gathering her thoughts went back to writing in her note pad. She looks up at me and I can tell she is back in therapist mode.

"What are you thinking about right now, Ariah?"

"How shocked you are. If anything, I want to know what you have written in that note pad about me. Is it that shocking to hear about me and Samuel's relationship?"

"Yes, it is, I never knew you two were that close. As your aunt I have many questions, but as your therapist I'm trying to hold back."

"Don't hold back. Ask whatever you want, I'll answer everything. That's why I'm here," I reassure her. It's silent for a moment. I can tell she's thinking about her first question and I know what that question will be.

"On your first day of school, when Charlie was out of town, why did you come home with ripped clothes and a bloody nose?" She pauses as if she's replaying that day in her head. "Was it Samuel who did that to you?"

"No, I'm sure he wasn't in town that day."

"I want to know what happened that day."

"Alright," I say as I close my eyes.

High school fucking sucked. I hated it and everyone around me. They were all like zombies that did nothing but follow. The only thing that mattered to these bastards was popularity. I never felt comfortable at school. If I were a fool daddy would have been right, coming here would have done nothing but undo all the shit he taught me for the past eight years. Everything that was being taught I had already learned, so it was easy to stay at the top of my class.

I started high school as a sophomore. I could have skipped a grade, but then what would have been the point? I was here to interact with snakes and have human relationships or whatever the fuck Shelly said. I didn't speak to anyone, and no one spoke to me. I just observed everything, soaking it all up like a sponge. This school was apparently for the rich and privileged, however if you asked me, it was a cesspool of garbage.

Sex, drugs, bribery and mind games could be found at every corner. The kids here were vicious and if you didn't have money, you were prey. I wasn't the only black kid, but there weren't many and on my first day of school I was taught a lesson I would never forget, 'take all threats seriously no matter how big or small, always strike first.' I was the new kid and people didn't know who I was or where I came from. The world knew Charles Blackwood had a daughter, but no one had ever seen her. I was not a socialite. I was always home reading or learning something. But on that first day of school, it wasn't until lunch time that someone finally approached me.

"Hey new girl, what's your name?" a tall guy in a letterman jacket came up and asked.

"If you want someone to give you their name, maybe next time provide yours first." I got up to leave, but he put his hand on my shoulder and pushed me back down. Oh, hell no, I thought. Pushing his hand off my shoulder, I sneered, "don't ever fucking touch me."

He raised his hand as if surrendering.

"My bad, I just wanted to know your name. I was thinking I could maybe show you how things work around

here. My name is Robert Maxwell, please accept my apology."
I ignored everything he said.

"Next time Robert, lead with that. And no thanks, I'm a smart girl I can figure this place out on my own." I walked away; I could see him walking back over to his group of friends. Walking to my next class, I was stopped by a group of girls in cheerleading outfits. "These must be the bitchy girls," I whispered to myself.

"Bitchy girls? Who are you calling bitchy?" a short black girl asked. She was the only black girl in the group, I guess she wanted to keep it that way.

"Hey slut, who the fuck are you and why were you talking to Alice's boyfriend?" Another girl asked as she pointed to a tall quiet girl in the back.

I exhaled, "who?"

"Robert, bitch you know who."

"I wasn't talking to him; he came over and started talking to me." I looked over at Alice, but she was still quiet. "Why the fuck am I explaining myself?" I said this more to myself.

"Nigger, watch yourself, he has a girlfriend. You're new so we're giving you a pass, but next time, we won't be so nice."

Whoa, time out. Was this the 1950's? Did she just call me a
nigger? I was beyond pissed, but not at her.

"So, you're gonna continue walking around with these
idiots after she just called me a nigger?" I stared at the short
black girl who had spoken to me first. Embarrassed, she
looked down at her shoes. We could have been friends, but
after that shit, fuck her ass too. My father taught me a long
time ago, that no matter what I do or how successful I
become, some people would only see the color of my skin. He
said it would always be the world against black people. My
godfather was in the room at the time, so I asked him, "well
what about John?" Before my father could answer, John
interjected.

"Baby girl, can't you see I'm black and beautiful?"
Daddy threw the pen he was holding in his hand at him. John
caught it and threw it right back. I smiled briefly at the
memory.

I pushed past the girls and headed to class. It was my
first day and I didn't want to create trouble. I had one more
class left before I was to meet Ryan, my driver/bodyguard in
front of the school. Walking down the hallway, I saw Robert
and his friends. My heart plummeted when I noticed he was

headed in my direction. At the other end of the hall, I see his girlfriend Alice, walking by herself, she stops dead in her tracks when she sees us.

"You still didn't tell me your name," Robert said, smirking. I openly glared at him.

"Look, stop playing games. Your girlfriend is right there. Stop trying to play with me because I'm new." I pushed past him, bumping his shoulder, he knew what he was doing by talking to me.

These motherfuckers wanted to play, fine. This was why I was here in the first place. Finishing my last class of the day I headed to my locker. Right away, I noticed it was open and all my things were on the floor. I picked my backpack up and closed my locker, the word "SLUT" was spray painted on the outside. I considered my choices. I could let it go and get bullied for the next three years or I could nip this shit in the bud today. I was mad at myself for not taking care of this earlier when she first threatened me, now I looked weak. My father would be disappointed. Blackwoods are not weak.

School was over, so I knew those bitches were somewhere practicing. I went straight into the girl's locker room. Since the school didn't have locks on the lockers, I opened each locker. It didn't matter who was involved, if your shit was in one of those lockers, I was cutting it up. I was pissed. I ripped all their shit to shreds. This still didn't make me feel better. I walked out the school and saw Ryan with a worried look on his face.

"Hey, Ariah, what took you so long? I was about to storm the school." This school was about to be a war zone.

"Open the trunk," I said not paying attention to him. Ryan opened the trunk and I walked over, grabbing a crowbar.

"Whoa, where are you going with that? What happened?" He stood in front of me.

"Move," I stated calmly. He grabbed his phone and moved out of my way. I knew he was probably calling my dad, but I didn't care, I was on a mission. I walked over to the parking lot that was next to the football field. I saw some cars parked over there. I figured they belonged to the football team and the cheerleaders. Trying to figure out which car belonged to whom would have taken all day. There were ten cars parked, so I smashed the windows of all of them. Ryan stood there watching, as Benny and Andrew, his back up, *pulled up. They watched the perimeter as I threw my tantrum.*

I was exhausted once I was finished with the last car. Practice must have finally been over, because I saw the football team walking out towards the parking lot first. I was sitting on top of someone's car catching my breath. Looking at all the damage, I felt good about all my hard work. Robert saw me and spoke first.

"Shit, new girl! What the fuck did you do to my new car?" I started laughing. I was happy that I was sitting on his Mustang. The cheerleaders ran towards the parking lot still in their uniforms.

"You fucking bitch!" Alice shouted, walking towards me.

"So now you can speak, cat let your tongue go?" I jumped off the car. One of the boys couldn't contain his anger and tried to attack me, but Ryan stopped him before he could get close. I yawned, now super tired from the work out I just had. All these angry faces staring at me made me excited.

"You did all this because of your locker?" the short black girl asked.

"No, I did all this to prove a point." I had done what I came to do and now I was ready to leave. I pushed my body off the hood of the car and looked at them. "I'm not to be fucked with."

"Fuck this," Alice said, running up on me. Yes, bitch come on, this was my first fist fight. She swung and punched me right in the nose, I immediately started bleeding. Fuck! That shit hurt. I had never been punched before, but right away I knew I never wanted to be punched again. I started punching back and managed to get my arms wrapped around her. Picking her body up, I slammed her to the ground. She was pulling at my clothes, trying to restrain me and keep my fist from hitting her face. I lost count of the number of punches I landed. Ryan, seeing my shirt had become ripped, pulled me off her. Once I was pulled off, Robert walked over and helped his girlfriend off the ground.

"You whore, my father will hear of this," Alice said. Her nose was bleeding, and her eyes and forehead looked bruised and swollen. I began laughing.

"I would like to thank you guys for my first high school experience." I'm sure I looked like a crazy woman. "Robert, you wanted to know my name so bad right?" He glared at me.

"Ariah Blackwood," I said, then turned and walked away. Fuck them and their threats, I wasn't afraid. Whoever their dads were, I knew mine was scarier. When I got home, I looked a mess. Shelly ran down the stairs, excited for me to tell her about my first day of school. Her eyes widened in alarm when she saw me, I looked at her and shrugged, "human relationships."

I begin laughing at the memory. Maybe I did go overboard. After I told them my name, they knew there was nothing they could do. My father is not a forgiving man and if any of their parents tried to come for me, they would lose everything. Charles Blackwood is far pettier than I am.

"Stop laughing, it's not funny. This whole time I thought you were assaulted," Dr. Blackwood says, annoyed.

"I'm sorry for never saying anything, I just didn't want daddy to find out." I stare at a painting on her wall. "There's no telling what he would have done."

"Yes, I know all too well. Alright, getting back on track, I apologize, that was something heavy on my heart. When you provided me the opportunity to ask, I took it."

"It's okay," I say, getting fidgety. "What's the next question?"

"How did you and Samuel's relationship start?" I feel myself becoming excited, and I hate myself for it.

The next two weeks of school were quiet. Now everyone knew my name and whose daughter I was. I assumed there would be consequences, but no one ever approached me. No one from the teaching staff even attempted to contact my dad. It was like it never happened.

The day was going fine, so I decided to eat lunch in the cafeteria. I found a table in the back and sat down facing the exit. I kept my headphones on, listening to music. Something told me to look up and when I did, Samuel walked through the doors. Our eyes met instantly; I only remember inhaling. I was staring and didn't care who noticed. Samuel walked in like he owned the place. My attraction to him was on some insane level. I could feel my mouth water, as I looked at his lips.

I watched him walk over to the football team's table. They eagerly made room for him. Ah there he is, the leader. I had to laugh to myself. Samuel was the same age as me, but he was the king of this school. That let me know right away, that these bastards were nothing but the gum on the bottom of my shoe. He had been gone on a business trip with my father and John, so he missed the first two weeks of school. I went back to eating my lunch, all the while pretending he didn't exist. Even though I was focused on my food, I could still feel someone looking right at me. By the time I looked up to see who the culprit was, a shadow covered me. Samuel was standing over me, staring down at me with an amused look on his face.

"I see you've been a naughty girl while daddy was away," his eyes never left mine.

"What did those little bitches do, run and tell? Wow, I'm so fucking scared." Samuel's stare was blank and emotionless, damn, he was intimidating.

"Whose daddy are you? Does John know you have a child?" My words sounded brave, but I couldn't meet his eyes. Whenever I was around him, I became someone I didn't recognize. My father and Shelly hadn't raised me to be weak, but here I was, quivering under his gaze. Samuel grabbed my chin and forced me to look up at him.

"Potty mouth, just like your father. You are far too beautiful to let such words leave your mouth. You want to be like him that bad?" I pushed his hand away.

"Fuck off, Samuel. You don't know me." I got up and walked away. That was an extremely sensitive subject for me.

As I was walking away, I heard him shout, "But I do, I know everything there is to know about you, Ariah." I refused to look back at his satisfied expression. I felt the beginnings of a panic attack and needed to find somewhere to calm down.

The night we met; I couldn't help myself. I told Samuel everything and anything he wanted to know about me. I was foolish, allowing myself to completely open up to a stranger. Like I said, I was different around him. Samuel asked me questions that no one else had, things everyone else wanted me to forget. He had listened so intently, making me feel as if he cared. Besides, it was not all my fault, he had me pinned down on the bed as he interrogated me. Samuel's face was too close, as he forced everything he wanted out of me. He could have asked me to marry him and I probably would have said yes. I even cried while lying under him. I was so stupid; I gave him all the ammo he needed to use against me.

I walked into the restroom and looked in the mirror. Fuck, I was blushing. This was the first time in my life I have ever felt like this. Before I met Samuel, I had felt alone, like no one knew me or even wanted to. He, for some reason, wanted to know everything about me. I threw some water on my face to wake myself up. I left the restroom just as the bell rung.

My phone begins ringing, "sorry, Shelly I have to take this." Looking at my phone, I see Chase's name pop up.

"Hello," I answer. The noise in the background is deafening.

"Babe I need some help. Can you meet me in the library in about 45 minutes?"

"Sure, I have a paper I need to finish anyway." I hang up, looking at Dr. Blackwood. "Why do I feel like we didn't really talk about much today, but I've been here for almost four hours."

She looks at me smiling, "I cannot tell you why you feel that way. We went over a lot; I think this was a good session. Call me anytime you want to talk."

I stand and stretch, releasing the tension from my body. Taking a deep breath, I begin grabbing my things. Walking out my aunt's office building, I feel refreshed again. I head toward the library, but I still have a bit of time before Chase arrives. I decide to go search for a book I need for my own homework. I love how Chase makes up excuses to have me help him study. I think it's cute. I stand in the aisle smiling as I look for the book.

"Who put that smile on your face?" I turn to see Samuel standing there staring at me. My whole body starts to throb, as if someone flipped a switch.

"Samuel," I say nervously. "Why are you here? Where's Chase?" I look around him, hoping to see Chase. The two of us cannot be alone, not again. There are no drunk idiots to stop him this time.

"Lover boy said he would be running late, he asked me to come keep you company. Keep the predators away," Samuel smiles as he starts walking towards me. I begin taking a few steps backward. "Lover boy is possessive and here I thought you didn't like being controlled." The closer he gets, the faster my heart beats. Now standing in front of me, I can feel his minty breath on my face. It is taking so much for me to keep myself from rubbing my body against his. How is he still able to do this to me?

"I don't know what you're talking about," I mumble. I try pushing him away, but his body doesn't budge. Just touching him sends electric currents through my hands. I close my eyes to keep myself calm.

"You don't?" His lips are inches away from mine. "Why did you leave me, Ariah?" I open my eyes. I don't know how to answer that. I'm becoming weak again, losing my resolve. Samuel tries to kiss me, but I turn away. I must keep my shit together. Chase will be here any minute, I don't need any misunderstandings. "Ariah, I'm getting upset," Samuel whispers in my ear.

This time I push him as hard as I can. The push creates enough space for me to squeeze by. Samuel grabs my arms, pulling me back to him. He is holding both of my arms as I face the bookshelf. My back is against his chest, his lips are once again next to my ear. Listening to him breathe is driving me to my breaking point. His warm breath causes tingles to run up and down my spine. My body starts to throb, it has been two years since I have been in his embrace, two years since I have wanted to be embraced.

"It looks like I have to remind your body of its owner after all," Samuel whispers. No, I can't let this happen. This asshole is manipulative, controlling, vindictive, narcissistic, arrogant, possessive and sadistic. Just say the fucking words, Ariah, I think to myself. Tell him. All I need to do is say four fucking words. It's too late. His hands have started moving, cupping my breast, he squeezes them. Samuel's lips are latched on to my neck, touching a spot that only he knows. I didn't realize how much I missed this. I throw my head back as a soft moan leaves my lips. One of his hands makes its way down to the top of my pants. With one hand he unbuttons them, and I find myself waiting in anticipation for what he is going to do next. Once his hand slides into my pants I inhale, my mind is turning to mush. Samuel doesn't move, his hand just sits there as my whole body continues to ache.

"Deep breaths baby, I know you missed me," he whispers while nibbling on my ear. He lightly kisses my neck, as he does this his hand slowly goes to work. "Just minutes and your underwear's ruined." His soft, breathy words in my ear is driving me insane. His hand moves faster, and I can feel myself about to explode. I close my eyes tightly, grabbing the arm that is wrapped around my shoulders. I bite into his arm to keep myself from screaming. His other hand is working my core round and round. My hips begin moving along with his hand. I become his instrument all over again. All movement stops and I know what's about to happen. My eyes start to water.

"Say the magic words, you know what I like to hear," Samuel says into my ear. He has me right where he wants me.

"Please, don't stop." I barely manage to get the words out, but it's what he needs to hear. Samuel starts right back where he left off, this time he's sucking harder on my neck and his hand is moving faster. I feel him bite down on my ear, hard, while his other hand squeezes my right breast. My body begins to tremble as my legs became weak. My body has left me behind and did what it wanted without my approval.

"From the looks of things, he hasn't touched you yet. I would be able to tell if my body had been touched." Samuel lets me go and my body falls to the floor. I look at the floor, tears in my eyes. Standing above me, he says in a deep low voice.

"You can never escape me. I will always find you. You belong to me." Samuel bends down, lifting my head so our eyes meet. "You wanted to play this game. You think you want Chase?" I have seen this look he has in his eyes before, it scared me then, it scares me now. "I'll play. It's been a while since you and I played. Don't you dare think of running away." He lets my face go and walks away. When he gets to the end of the aisle, he turns back, looking over his shoulder. "Lover boy should be on his way, enjoy your study date."

I have got to be the worst bitch on the planet. I send Chase a text telling him that I'm not feeling well. I need to get out of here. I can't let Chase see me hot and bothered by another man. I care for him too much to hurt him. I hate the person I've become for Samuel, the submissive dummy. I refuse to be his or anyone else's plaything. I want to be someone's equal; Chase makes me feel like I am his equal and not a toy.

Chapter Five

The next morning, I wake up feeling refreshed. I could smack myself; did I need an orgasm that fucking bad? Getting out of bed, I pick my phone up looking at it, no messages. I guess Chase was fine with me blowing him off yesterday. Maybe I should go visit him today to make it up to him. I get in the shower, trying my hardest to clean my tainted body. I should blame Samuel for the way I feel right now, but that would be too easy. I allow him to treat me the way he does, so I'm trash as well. I won't let it happen again.

I have a couple classes today, but they start later in the afternoon. So, my plan is to buy breakfast and wake Chase up. Walking up his walkway reminds me of the night Samuel came back into my life. I shake my head; I need to focus. I am about to see Chase and I want to give him all my attention. Before I can make it up to the porch of the frat house, the front door flies open, out walks the random girl from the party that had been all over Chase. The girl's clothes are a mess, she looks like she was rushed out the house.

Looking towards the doorway, I see Samuel. He's leaning against the door shirtless; his basketball shorts hang low on his hips. His hands were just in my pants, I guess I'm not enough. Fuck, I have to catch myself, I sound jealous. Samuel is not mine; Chase is. Yes, Chase, let's focus, Ariah.

Walking into the house, I brush past Samuel, trying my hardest to make sure our bodies don't touch.

"No good morning kiss?" he asks, while smiling like an idiot.

"Go kiss your whore, you know, the one you just walked out the door."

"Oh, babe you sound jelly, if yo-".

Before he can finish, I flip him off, heading up stairs. My mind is on one thing and one thing only, Chase. I walk right into his room. It's clean with everything in its rightful place. I hear the shower running, I drop my bag then place his breakfast on his desk. Plopping down on his bed, I begin getting lost in diner dash. After about ten minutes, I hear the shower turn off, right after that Chase walks into the room in just a towel.

"Shit babe, you scared me," he says, looking at me then over to the food. Forgetting about me, he walks over to his desk.

I laugh at how cute he looks attacking the breakfast sandwiches while only in a towel. "Chase, don't you want to get dressed first?"

"Oh yeah," he puts the food down, then walks over to his closet. "So, I talked to my mom, and she wants us to come over tomorrow for dinner. That is, if you still want to go." Chase walks out of his closet fully dressed. I don't remember telling him I would go. I guess if meeting his parents is going to stop them from introducing him to hoes, I can do this. I don't know if I love Chase, but I care for him deeply. I want us to work.

"Alright Chase." I stand up, ready to leave. I want to go to the library and finish the assignment that I couldn't complete yesterday. Before I can pick my bag up, Chase pulls me to him for a deep kiss. I fight every urge I have to push him away and for the first time in our relationship, I let Chase hold me for as long as he wants.

When he finally releases my lips, my back is against the wall with my legs wrapped around him. I am so focused on him that I have no idea what is happening. This is the first time someone other than Samuel has made me feel like this. I smile as we both stare at each other, breathing heavily. I feel my body tingle a little, I feel butterflies in my stomach, I feel myself blush. Looking into Chase's eyes while he holds me in his arms, I feel a sexual attraction to him. It feels good being this close to him.

"Fuck, I have class in ten," he grunts, letting me down.

"I also have to finish a paper," I say, panicked. I pick my bag up and rush out of his room. My heart is racing in excitement. I am falling for Chase on my own. Making it out the frat house and down the walkway, I bump into a girl I had never seen before. I'm so excited that I'm not paying attention to what is in front of me.

"Oh, I'm sorry," I say, turning to continue on my merry way.

"Of course, you are bitch!" I turn back around to make sure I heard her correctly. She is standing in the middle of the sidewalk, glaring at me. One would think I killed her grandma or something. Is she challenging me? I have never seen this girl in my life. Now none of that matters, she has my full attention. I walk right up to her.

"You sure you got the right person?" Even if she apologizes, after her next words, she is getting decked. Before she can answer my question, the front door opens, and both Samuel and Chase walk out. I don't pay much attention to them; I'm still staring at the girl waiting for an answer. I can feel Samuel's eyes on me, Chase on the other hand is looking at the girl. This pisses me off even more, who is this bitch?

The girl smiles, "yeah I got the right p-." Before she can finish her sentence, I punch her right in the nose. I can hear my father's words in my head, "disrespect will never be tolerated". I don't know this girl and I don't care. She stands up from the ground holding her nose, she looks over to Chase and Samuel.

"So, you're just gon' stand there and let her hit me like this?" Who is she talking to? I know it better not be Chase. Who is this bitch?

Samuel walks up to her. "Brittany come on, let's get some ice on that." He walks her into the frat house. I should have known; Samuel always had a way with hoes. But why was she coming at me over him? He has free rein; she can have him. Chase walks over to me, laughing.

"Look at bae with the mean left." He takes my hand, massaging it. We start making our way to campus. I tell Chase about what happen, but he keeps laughing. Making it to the library, Chase kisses my cheek, then runs to class. Luckily, I finish my paper plus some homework I've been putting off. I still have two hours left before my class. I look at my phone, I have two missed calls from my father. Deciding I should call him back before he gets mad and just shows up, I dial his number.

"Hi daddy," I say with an eye roll.

"Young lady, don't roll your eyes at me." I stop walking, how did he know? I look around and there he stands with his guards in tow. He is staring right at me, I hang up the phone and run straight over to him, hugging him as tight as I can.

"Daddy," I say happily, he tries to push me off, but I won't let him.

"So, you have to see me in person for you to treat me like I'm your father? I've been calling you for a week." All I can do is smile as he scolds me. I know what he wants to talk about but seeing him makes me forget about all of that. I don't care that I look like a little girl, or that people are looking at us. I love my father and I missed him very much.

"Come on let's go, I'm hungry. I was too angry to eat on the flight," he grumbles. Taking my hand, we walk over to his car. I stare at him; it has been a whole year since I last saw him. My father is still handsome, looking younger than his age. I grab his arm, leaning my head on his shoulder. He never complains about how clingy I am towards him. He never cared that I would sit in a corner as quiet as a mouse just to be near him.

"Did you tell Shelly you were here?"

"No, Ariah I did not. I didn't know I was coming," he says, looking out the window. I can tell he's annoyed I haven't been communicating with him. In his mind, I'm basically defying him. I hope he understands that I'm just going through my own things. I know he wants me to finish school so I can join Blackwood Inc. and work under him. I will end up doing just that, but I want to take my time. This could have been my last year of school, but I stretched my classes out. I want to be normal for just a bit longer, not

Ariah Blackwood, just Ariah. We pull up outside my aunt's office.

"Stay here," he says, getting out the car.

I sit there for about twenty minutes, before deciding to pull out my paper to read it over. As much as I want to get out and go see what the hell is keeping them, I don't want to make my father more upset by not listening to him. He jumped on a flight just to come talk to me, which means he's probably leaving tonight.

Both car doors open at the same time, and I look up to see my dad and aunt getting in on either side. I look over at my aunt, and her face lights up with a smile. Shelly grabs my hand and squeezes it affectionately. I look at my father, he seems calmer. I take his hand, laying my head on his shoulder. We don't talk. We just stay in that position as the vehicle rumbles to a start. I must admit, the silence is comforting.

Oh, how I hate Mondays! Rolling over in my bed, I look up at my ceiling; maybe I should add some art. After lunch with Shelly and my father, I came straight home. My father informed me that next semester will be my last. He has made adjustments to my schedule and I am to follow it. He has also made me aware that he knows about my relationship with Chase and he doesn't approve. Apparently, Chase isn't good enough for me. I'm livid. How dare he? There was so much tension in that restaurant that I just left. Charles Blackwood is a control freak and I hate that he's always right.

He's skilled at reading people and he knows me better than anyone else. I hope he's wrong about Chase. No, I know he's wrong. Chase is amazing, and if he makes me feel amazing, he's here to stay. My thoughts shift to Chase. How will he handle the prospect of me leaving in a few months? Maybe I could talk him into coming with me. I rub my forehead in frustration as I feel the beginnings of a migraine.

Getting out of bed, I text Shelly letting her know I plan on stopping by. I feel like I'm finally getting Samuel out of my system. I'm opening up to Chase more and I know it has something to do with our sessions. Shelly texts me back letting me know that my stopping by is fine. Today I will tell her everything, I need to just get rid of it all.

Lying on Dr. Blackwood's couch, looking up at the ceiling, I replay all the memories I have of Samuel. I hear her clearing her throat, letting me know that she's ready whenever I am. Am I ready? Will I ever be? There is so much to tell, so many wounds to rip open.

Today was just like any other day. I walked into school; people stared but said nothing, just the way I liked it. As usual, there was nothing worth my attention being taught in my classes. Seeing the same people day in and day out had made me dread coming to this place. I could have told my father that I didn't want to come here anymore, but I'm not a quitter. I started this, and I plan to finish it. Walking into the cafeteria, I sat at my usual table alone with my headphones glued to my ears. A few minutes later, someone sits next to me. I don't even bother to look up, since my plan is to ignore them. I jerked in surprise when warm hands wrap around my waist and began pulling me. I knew who it was without looking up since only one person ever spoke to me.

"What do you want? Can't you see I'm busy?" I had gotten use to him touching me. Not that I had a choice when it came to him. Even if I pushed him away, he wouldn't let go. Samuel was the kind of guy who went after what he wanted and held on tight.

"I just want to be close to you. Even if you lie to yourself, you can't lie to me." I turned and looked into his eyes. Samuel was right, I wanted to be close to him. From the moment I first saw him, I liked him. I would never admit it, because then he would own me, body and soul. Usually, I would have gotten up and walked away from him. But as I looked into his eyes, I wanted to try something different.

"You know, if you were my boyfriend, you could be as close to me as you want." Samuel looked down at the table. I smiled inwardly, just as I thought. He only wanted someone to play with. Every now and then, sure, I would partake in his petty games, but not when it came to my body. I would not be a notch on his belt or some girl he could add to his list. If he wanted me, he could have me as long as I was the only dish being served at the table. Tired of the games, I pushed him off *me and got up to leave. This was a scene that happened daily. I would be sitting at lunch, minding my business, and he would appear, whispering in my ear. Then I would push him away and leave. This happened so often that people were taking bets on how long it would take me to push him away. Normally, Samuel would laugh it off and walk back over to his friends, but not this day.*

"Ariah, I want you to be my girlfriend," Samuel spoke clearly and loudly so everyone would hear him. I turned around, looking at him. He had a determined look on his face, one that let me know he was serious. He started walking towards me, I stood there in shock, Samuel Conrad wanted a girlfriend. What he was doing was so out of character.

"So now what, Ariah? I'm asking you to be mine. I've tried to contain myself, kick back and go with the flow of things, but you won't let that happen. You were mine the moment I laid eyes on you, the moment I cared and wanted to know everything about you. Me asking you right now is just a formality." I blushed at his declaration. I was proud and arrogant; I dropped my gaze for no one. But right now, in front of Samuel I felt defeated. Staring into my eyes, his soft

voice commanded me, "I want to hear you say it. I want to hear you say that you're mine."

Without hesitation, the words slipped from my mouth, "I'm yours."

"Forever," Samuel finished. He gently kissed my lips. It felt magical and final, as if I had just sealed my fate. Then without a word, he walked back over to his table. I ran out of the cafeteria, flushed and ecstatic.

"The moment I told that asshole I was his, I was. Samuel taught me many things. Actually, we taught each other many things. But the thing that stuck with me from Samuel, was that words mean things."

"Is that not something everyone knows?" Dr. Blackwood asked.

I continue staring at the ceiling, "Not like Samuel. He uses them as a buffer, my words could stop him or make him move forward."

"Give me an example," she asked.

Samuel and I had been dating for about a month. To be honest, nothing had really changed between us. He would walk up to me, grab my waist and kiss me like it was his last time. Even though everyone in school knew we were together, no one said a word. But being with Samuel came with rules.

Rule #1: Anytime, whether day or night, my phone rang, or I received a text from him, I was to answer it immediately.

Rule #2: I wasn't allowed to hang around any other guys.

Rule #3: If at any time, Samuel and I were getting intimate with each other and I was uncomfortable, all I had to do was tell him these 4 words: "I don't want this."

The third rule pleased me, because I knew it was as a result of everything I had told him about my past. He was so attentive when it came to me and my feelings that it amazed me sometimes. The rules were easy for me to follow. I didn't talk or hang out with anyone, and I always had my phone on me. However, this is the real world, so when everything is going well, something bad must happen, right? I could never just enjoy being a normal high school girl with her boyfriend. Robert somehow managed to corner me in the hallway one day.

"So, you and Samuel?"

"Yep, me and Samuel, now if you'll excuse me." I tried to push past him, instead he wrapped his arms around me. Pushing him off, I looked up to see Alice holding a camera with a smirk on her face. Neither of them said a word as they walked away. I knew what they planned to do with those pictures, but what I didn't know was how Samuel would react. Samuel was not king at this school for nothing. If these assholes wanted to play games, he would play right along with them. He didn't care how he won, just that he won.

Samuel's last name didn't make people fear him like mine did. It was the things that Samuel himself would do that made him king. I tried calling him, but his phone went straight to voice mail. During that time of day, I knew he would be in the library. As I walked into the library, sure enough there he was packing his things up, ready to leave.

"Hey," he looked up at me and smiled. "I was just on my way to you." He pulled me in for a hug.

"I tried to call you, but your phone is dead." He smirked playfully.

"Someone took it during third period. I wonder why?" He took my hand and smiled. "Someone wants to play, so whatever you're in a rush to tell me, don't. Let's not ruin the

surprise. It would seem they worked hard on it." My eyes widened at his reasoning. Yep, he was crazy as hell. I felt a twinge of pity for them because I knew, no matter what, it would have a bad ending. I didn't have time to worry about them though, I needed to worry about myself.

"Okay, fine. But you have to promise me you won't get mad at me." I shivered at the small smile on his face.

"Come on babe, let's go see the show." We walked into the cafeteria and you could hear a pin drop. Something had everyone's attention, so of course, we walked over to see what was going on. I inhaled.

"As you can see, she still wants him. I heard her myself trying to get my boyfriend to be with her. She has her own boyfriend, so why does she want mine? Just because her father is Charles Blackwood she thinks she can do whatever she wants." Alice deserved a fucking Oscar. She was crying dramatically, her faithful minions huddled around her. One would have thought her mother had just died. Apparently, one of Alice's friends told her they wanted to show her something, and it just so happened to be the picture of me and Robert. This picture was different from what happened.

In this picture, Robert and I were kissing. Robert stepped forward and took the phone from the friend.

"Babe, you know I love you. I would never try to hurt you. She kissed me." I wanted to laugh so hard, but I couldn't because my hand was being squeezed tightly. Before I could say anything, Samuel let my hand go then walked over to Robert and took his phone. Samuel looked at the phone, then at me. The glare he gave me made me shiver. I turned around to leave, this was too much.

When did they have time to fix the picture? It really looked like we were kissing. I was over it, over all the drama and back biting that came with being in high school. That night, Samuel didn't call or text and I cried myself to sleep. I had tried to tell him what had happened, but he'd refused to let me.

The next day everyone glared at me as I walked by, but I didn't care. Fuck them. I hadn't seen Samuel, but as far as I was concerned, fuck him too. If he wanted to believe them without even asking me what happened, so be it. He claimed he knew me better than I knew myself, so what the fuck? Leaving class and heading toward the library, I saw Alice. She looked at me, a bright smile on her face. I gave my fakest smile. I was two seconds away from fucking her world up. My phone chimed and I dismissed her, checking to see who it was. My heart leapt when I saw it was Samuel asking me to meet him. I headed to the cafeteria, but when I got there, a projector was set up and Samuel was standing next to it.

"Yesterday, we watched a play, so how about today we watch a movie?" Samuel spoke loudly so everyone could hear him. He had everyone's attention and the creepiest smile on his face. When his eyes found mine in the crowd, he winked. Robert and the football team walked in with Alice and her crew right behind them.

"It's good that you guys could join us. After the performance you guys put on yesterday, I went home and thought, how could I top that? What could I possibly do?" Samuel walked over, grabbed Robert by his shoulders, led him over to a chair and sat him down.

"Hey man, we get it, you're mad. It was a joke," Robert's voice was nervous and shaky.

"But did anybody laugh?" Samuel looked at me. "Babe, did you think what happened yesterday was funny?" I shook my head. "Why don't we get this party started." Samuel pressed play on the projector. Apparently, Alice and Robert liked to partake in the same hobbies. No wonder they went together so well, they both liked dicks in their mouths. They liked looking into each other's eyes as their tongues intertwined on someone's penis. This was some weird shit. How did Samuel even get this video? Of course, Robert tried to attack Samuel, but the football team held him back. Alice sat in the corner and cried real tears this time.

"Well, I guess what you two have is true love." Samuel's booming laughter echoed against the walls. The whole cafeteria was quiet. Everyone was just trying to unsee the grotesque images from the screen. I was focused only on Samuel, was he still mad at me? I tried to walk over to him, but he walked away. Ryan picked me up from school that day.

"Hey, is my father home?" I asked.

"No, I just dropped him and Mr. Conrad off at the airport."

"Take me to Sam's house," I said staring out the window. Ryan knew about us; I didn't care as long as he kept it from my father. Arriving at the Conrad estate, I walked up to the large door and hesitated. What was I nervous about? Before I could decide if I wanted to knock or not, the door swung open. Samuel stood there, staring at me. I tried to step inside, but he blocked me.

"If you come inside, you aren't leaving tonight." I looked away from him, getting the gist of what he meant. "You should get in the car and go home." Finding my nerve, I looked up at him. Samuel's eyes looked like they were begging me to leave. Like he really didn't want me to go inside. Without thinking, I walked up to him, this time he moved letting me in. He closed the door behind me.

"Ariah, don't forget rule number three." Remembering rule number three was useless, I knew what I was doing. I knew what I wanted. Samuel took my hand, leading me through his home and up to his bedroom. This was not my first time in his room, but it felt like it. The last time I was in Samuel's room, I hadn't gotten the chance to look around, and from the way his hands were on me, it looked like I wouldn't be looking around this time either. I didn't have time to register what was happening, before I knew it, I was roughly tossed on the bed. Samuel got on top of me using his legs to spread mine. I closed my eyes as flashes of heavy hairy stomachs flickered through my head. Men that I did not know hovered over my small curled up body. Why was this memory *surfacing at a time like this? I didn't want to remember my horrid past. I felt the tears forming and my throat started to constrict.*

"Ariah." I opened my eyes. "Look at me," Samuel says directly above me. "Look right at me. Do not mistake me for anybody else." He kissed my nose. "Watch everything that I am about to do to you. You control the outcome; you know what to say." I nodded my head, telling myself that I controlled the outcome. "Breathe Ari, I don't want you fainting on me. Take deep breaths." I did as he said.

Chapter Six

"So, you ended up having consensual sex with Samuel?"

"Yes," I say, picking up the glass of water sitting in front of me.

"Did you regret it? Is that why you ran away?" I exhale.

"Regret, no. In fact, I felt the complete opposite. I wanted to stop when I started having flashbacks, but he forced me to watch, to see that it was him. He wouldn't let me run away, he made me think I was in control."

"What do you mean by made you think? From what you just told me, if you would have just told him that you didn't want to have sex, it wouldn't have happened."

I begin laughing. "Back then, Samuel could have asked anything of me. He did actually ask anything of me, and I would never refuse him. He tells me I have control but pins me down to his bed and forces me to tell him my life story. Even if I were mad at him, he would force me to talk to him about it. When I was afraid to have sex, he forced me to get over it." I run my hands through my hair. "Samuel makes me feel like I want to do all these things, but I feel like I'm playing right into his hands. I don't have time to think anything through, shit just happens. And when it's all said and done, I never regret it. In fact, I just want him more." I sit back and look at the ceiling. "When I was with Samuel, I felt like my body and my mind wasn't mine, like I was his puppet. You think I'm being dramatic, right? It's fine, I understand how it sounds. But it's the first time I'm saying these feeling out loud."

"I don't think you're being dramatic. What I think does not matter, how you feel does." I sit back up, looking at my aunt.

"That sounds like something he said to me once. Samuel doesn't like secrets, if it's about me, he wants to know it all."

It was my last year of high school, we had been together for about eighteen months. We had a system, in school we were all over each other, but outside of school we would have to meet privately. This was not something hard to do, since my father and John were always gone on business. I'd been thinking lately that I had no freedom, I felt like I couldn't think or do anything for myself.

My father had already planned my life out for me. I knew what I was going to do for the rest of my life, it was too late to turn back. In my relationship, I was a puppet. I stopped answering texts or calls from Samuel and I began giving my father the silent treatment. This upset them both. One morning, while having breakfast I guess Charles Blackwood had had enough.

"Ariah, what the fuck is wrong with you?" he asked, putting his fork down to give me his full attention. I didn't say anything. It didn't help that Shelly had moved away and hadn't told me why. She was the buffer between he and I, and now she was gone.

"Young lady, I know you hear me talking to you."

"I'm just living my life the way you want me to." The words flew out of my mouth.

"I thought something was going on, you had me worried. If I'm not mistaken you chose to live like this. As a matter of fact, you were sitting right in that seat when you

said it." My father picked his fork up and continued to eat, with no regard for my feelings.

I got even more pissed, I felt like he was blowing me off. In my seventeen years of life, I had never gotten angry with him. How could he take the words of a seven-year-old so seriously? As I thought about it, I calmed down and started laughing. I remember him telling me that there was no turning back and not to even speak those words to him. I chose to live like this, I had asked to be his protege.

After breakfast I went to school. I was still having a hard time letting go of my frustration. Samuel walked up to me, his face clouded with anger. He took my hand and pulled me outside. After pushing me into the passenger seat of his car, he got in and drove off. The car ride was quiet, neither of us said a word. I didn't care about leaving school, I hadn't wanted to be there anyway. We ended up driving down some dirt road that led us to a cabin. When I stepped out of the car, I was hit with the smell of fresh pine.

"Where are we?" I asked looking around. Though it was a cabin, surrounded by forest, it looked like a middle-class home. It was modernized, with a remote two door garage and paved driveway. It looked to be at least two stories. Why was such a beautiful home in the middle of nowhere?

"This is my house. I won it in a bet against my father. Believe it or not, he makes me work for everything, nothing is free."

"Why did you bring me here?"

"You looked like you have a lot to say, so let's go in so we can talk without interruption." I followed him into the cabin, the place was beautiful. I could tell that all the furniture was new. Once he closed the door, he stared at me.

"What happened? Why haven't you been answering my texts or phone calls?" I sighed.

"I think we should break up." I began to tell him how I felt like I was his puppet, a rag doll he tossed around as he pleased. How I wanted to take control, real control of my own life and my body. After my rant, he stared at me quietly. I stared at him, trying unsuccessfully to gauge his reaction. The house was quiet, too quiet. I nervously fiddled with my fingers. The way he stared at me made me feel unsure of myself.

"Fine Ariah, you want to be my victim? Then so be it. You want me to be the villain? I'll be your villain. But a puppet master?" He paced back and forth, his fingers curled tightly into a fist. "Have you forgotten that I know what happened to you? I came up with a rule especially for you. I didn't want you to feel pressured, but I'm also not about to allow you to compare me to a fucking pedophile."

Samuel began walking towards me and instinctively I backed up. I didn't know what he was going to do, but I couldn't be close to him. If he were too close, I knew I would give in. My back was to a wall, while he stood right in front of me. I felt my knees become weak; I could hear my heartbeat. I tried looking away, but he turned my face back to his.

"Break up? Even if we break up, you'll still be mine. You think I'm playing around with you? Pulling strings?" Samuel kissed my lips. "I hear you loud and clear, Ariah. Your feelings matter to me. Don't keep anything from me ever, no matter what it is. If it's about you, I want to know." He kissed me deeply, his hands roamed all over my body. I clung to him for dear life, falling deep into the warmth of him. But suddenly he pulled away.

"Let's go. I don't want to force you into anything." He took my hand, but I snatched it away from him. I was breathing heavily; I'm sure my cheeks were red. Samuel had *aroused me on purpose. He was trying to prove a point, fucking bastard.*

"What? You don't want to go back to school?"

"No, I don't want to go back to school," I answered desperately.

"Well, what is it you want to do? Because after your little break up rant, I'm not touching you until you beg me to." He pushed me up against the wall. "I want you to be absolutely sure that I'm what you want."

"That was the beginning of my punishment."

"Punishment?" Dr. Blackwood asks with raised eyebrows.

"According to Samuel, I had hurt him deeply. He said I basically accused him of rape. So, if I wanted to have sex or an orgasm, I'd have to ask him for it."

"So, did you ask him," she clears throat. "for your orgasms?"

"Sure did. I thought it was a thing that would eventually pass, but after that day, he became a sadist and I his little obedient masochist. Samuel began to take pleasure in bullying me, especially during sex. And I loved it." My aunt looks at me, I know what she is thinking. "You think

I'm a hypocrite? I do too. I say I'm a puppet and that Samuel is pulling all the strings, making me feel weak. But then I tell you how I loved the way it felt, how he made me feel. This is my dilemma; I don't want to feel like this for Samuel anymore. Too much has happened. I don't want to go back. I want to move forward with Chase."

"Chase? He's the guy your father was talking about?"

"Yes, he and I have been dating for almost two years. I'm going to meet his parents tonight. These sessions have helped me. I feel like I'm finally getting Samuel out of my system and opening up more to Chase."

"Before we get to Chase, Ariah, why did you come here, to California I mean?" I stare at my aunt as my latest trauma surfaces.

It was a month before graduation, I didn't know if I was going to college or not. My father had told me it didn't matter what I decided. I knew I never wanted to see these people again. It was no longer fun being here. I'd had my fun, now I wanted to move on. Samuel and I didn't break up, but lately he had become super distant. Whenever we were together, all we did was have sex. I'd ask him what was wrong, and he would smile and pretend everything was fine.

I assumed he was just thinking about his future. One thing we both knew was that there would probably be no happy ending for us. We were both products of our fathers, so whatever they said was all that mattered. My father wanted me to marry for business; Samuel would take over for his father which meant he would probably work for me, so he was not a candidate. We both knew this, but never talked about it. I didn't want to talk about it, I just wanted to be with him, right there in the moment. My future was not mine to look forward to, so I wanted to enjoy the present. I wanted to enjoy Samuel. A few weeks before school ended, there was a party. In the three years that I had been attending high school, I had never attended a party. So, I figured, why not? Maybe this would lighten Samuel's mood.

I woke up that morning not feeling very well. Running straight to the bathroom, I threw up. I brushed it off, thinking maybe I had eaten too much. But the feeling continued throughout the day. No matter what I ate, it came right back up. My father was gone, and Shelly was all the way in California. One of the maids gave me some crackers and a coke, which surprisingly stayed down. I called Samuel to see if we would be going together or meeting up there, but he didn't answer. Instead, he sent me a text telling me he would meet me there. I went into my aunt's room to find a dress to wear; I didn't have any tight dresses, but I knew she did.

I had my hair up in a high ponytail to show off my neckline in the dress. I did listen to Shelly when she would blabber about fashion. I wore a tight black dress that stopped mid-thigh, with diamond studded pumps. I found them at the back of Shelly's closet, they were in a clear case sitting under a spotlight, like a treasure. Looking at myself in the mirror, I knew Samuel would lose his shit when he saw me. I grabbed my clutch and headed for the door. I wanted the night to be fun, it was my first and last high school party.

"Hey Ryan, stay close I'm not sure we will be here long." Ryan looked at me through the rear-view mirror and nodded his head. I took a deep breath and moved toward the house.

When I walked through the unfamiliar house, all eyes were on me. I knew no matter what I chose I could not go wrong with raiding Shelly's closet. I could hear the whispers of girls saying that the diamonds on my shoes were real. Ridiculous, granted we were rich, but why would my aunt have shoes with real diamonds on them? Tired of walking *around, I decided to ask one of the random girls if they had seen Samuel.*

"Hey, have you seen Samuel around here?"

She looked at me, "yeah I saw him go upstairs with Paris like fifteen minutes ago." Paris? Who the fuck was that? I headed upstairs, curious to find out where he was. I tried to open a random door, but it was locked. Going to a second door, I was greeted with the sight of two horny teens making out. I was jealous, I wanted to be making out. Where the fuck was Samuel? Going to another door, the knob turned, and I peeked my head inside. And there he sat with some blond I had never seen before on his lap. I stepped inside the room, closed the door and turned the lock. Two sets of eyes stared at me. I found a desk chair, pulling it in front of the door, I took a seat.

"Excuse me, we are kind of busy," dumb blond had the nerve to have an attitude. Samuel sat there looking at me, he had a beer in his hand, so he was probably drunk.

"Hey Paris, this is my amazing girlfriend, Ariah. You know, daughter of Charles Blackwood, heir to a throne all of her own." Samuel took swig of his beer. The girl didn't say a word, but her face fell as she glanced between the two of us.

Maybe she hadn't known he had a girlfriend. I sat there quietly, but my blood boiled. I was ready to lash out and fight them both. But I also wanted an explanation. Why was he using this girl to push me away? The unconditional trust I had in him had now been shattered. He started laughing.

"Are you going to sit there and block us in? By the way, you look really fucking sexy right now. I would ask you to join us, but I know that won't happen."

"Should I leave and allow the two of you to continue?" I asked sarcastically. Samuel was no longer amused.

"She speaks, the queen speaks," he shouted.

"What the fuck is your problem? Why are you acting like some insecure piece of shit? What? Did someone tell you that we couldn't be together? Did someone say we wouldn't work? What the fuck!" He looked away; his mouth pinched into a tight line. If someone did in fact say something like that to him, it could only be one person. "Did John find out about us?" This time he threw his beer bottle up against the wall causing blondie to jump.

"Hey, let me just leave," she pleaded. I didn't move.

"No, I don't want to be alone with him. You have to wait until we're finished talking." I looked over at Samuel, he

looked like shit. "He told you to leave me alone? Does that mean you have to listen? We've been doing what we want so far, why does it have to change?"

Samuel smirked. "You know just like I do, we can't make those kinds of choices for ourselves. We are living the life that they want us to. If Charles found out and he told you we couldn't be together, what would you do?" He was right, we didn't have the freedom to live how we wanted.

"I don't know what I would do, but I wouldn't do this. I would put more distance between us, sure, but I would talk to you about it. Who was it that said, no secrets, talk to each other no matter what?" I could feel the tears as they started to gather behind my eyes. "I would have fought for us." I got up, pushing the chair out the way. Before I could open the door, Samuel pushed it closed.

"Where are you going? We're not done talking."

"Yes, we are. I can't trust you anymore. I'm leaving." I tried to move his hands.

"Leaving? You can't leave me. This," he pointed at me then himself. "is forever."

"You're drunk, fuck off," I said struggling to get him out the way. Pushing him with force, I finally made it out the room. I almost made it to the top of the stairs when Samuel grabbed my hand, trying to pull me back.

"Ariah, you can't leave me. I own you mind, body and soul," he shouted.

"Well motherfucker, you should have thought about that before you decided to act like a little bitch and hook up with some whore." By this point, the music had stopped playing and everyone was looking at us.

"You can't leave me. I won't let you, not now, not ever." The look in Samuel's eyes scared me. I just wanted to get out of there. He had no right to demand anything from me, not anymore. I snatched my arm away from him and lost my footing. I fell down the stairs hard, I felt each step as I went down. I didn't hit my head, but my torso hurt so badly that I thought maybe I had broken a rib. Fuck, my father was going to kill me, I thought. Samuel ran down the stairs and picked me up. I didn't want him touching me, but I was too weak to protest. Rushing outside he called for Ryan, who was standing around with the other drivers. Once he heard his name, he threw away his cigarette and got the car.

We couldn't go to a hospital because I was afraid my father would find out. He was not supposed to get back to *town until next week. Samuel decided to take me back to my house and called his family doctor. When he was getting me out the car, we realized there was blood coming down my legs. I became hysterical so all the maids came to help. I made them promise to never speak of that night to anyone.*

Once the doctor finished my check up and prescribed me some medicine, I fell asleep. I woke up to Samuel holding me in his arms, crying. I started crying as well. I'd had a miscarriage. I looked around my room and saw that all the equipment was gone. The bloody sheets had been changed, the dress that I was wearing gone, the only thing left of that night were the diamond studded heels sitting of my vanity.

To be honest, I wasn't sure why I was crying, so many sad things were happening to me at once. The one person on the planet who knew the real me would have allowed me to be a single mother. He wouldn't fight for me like I would for him. The child that he and I made would never breathe fresh air. We were seventeen and our reality had been shit, just like my mother once told me.

I hear sobs coming from Dr. Blackwood. She stands, walks over to the couch and sits next to me. I exhale as she pulls me in for a hug.

"Umm, Dr. Blackwood, I don't think this is professional," I say through my own tears.

"Why didn't you say anything? What the fuck, Ariah? We could have been there for you. You always go through things alone."

"If I would have said something, Samuel, and John for that matter, would probably be dead. That's why you can never let him find out. Never." Finally getting herself together, she gently holds my hand. "When daddy returned, I told him I wanted to come to California with you and go to college. He was sad at first, then he agreed. So here I am. I don't want to run anymore. Leaving Samuel was one of the hardest things I've ever done. But we were kids trying to handle grown up situations."

"Well, you're here now, you have Chase. You can move on."

"That's the thing." I look at her nervously. "The reason I have been here almost every day is because he found me. Samuel is here, going to my school and he's friends with Chase."

Chapter Seven

"What do you mean he's here and friends with Chase?" The look on Shelly's face is one of pure confusion. "How the hell did he find you? How does he know Chase? What the fuck? When did all this happen? Was he the reason you decided to have these sessions?" I place my hands on her shoulders.

"Please calm down. I don't know the answers to these questions you're asking me. I just know he's here, turning my world upside down." I sigh, sitting back.

"My emotions are a whirlwind. I was trying so hard to get him out of my system, then poof out of nowhere he appears. I am ridiculous, even now I can't help but remember the way his hands felt on my body. Samuel is an addiction. But we're toxic together, we have no future together, and yet I can't help but be drawn to him. I try to blame him for how I feel, but I know it's not his fault. Since I left, I've been trying to find words that could best explain how I feel. I can't find them." I look at Shelly, she's staring at me as if she understands where I'm coming from. How could she, how could anyone?

"For some time, I tried to say that it was love. Then Chase came along and made me feel different things. He makes me feel so comfortable, with him I feel safe. He allows me to take my time, he gives me space to think things through. I'm not forced; my emotions are not forced out of me. I don't feel cornered." I sigh. "I get so mad at myself for holding back. In my mind, I want to give Chase all of me, I want to let him in. But I'm scared." My eyes begin to water as my insecurity reveals itself. "What if the tainted me isn't good enough for him? What if the way he looks at me changes?" I roll my eyes, taking a deep breath. "If daddy were here, he'd be so disappointed at how weak I sound. This is fucking embarrassing."

Shelly gets up and walks back over to her desk. I can tell she is back in Dr. Blackwood mode. "Ariah, why do you compare Chase to Samuel?"

"Samuel is all I know," I answer, shrugging.

"Why did you open up to him the first time you met him?" I look at the painting on the wall behind her.

"I've always wanted someone to care, to ask what happened to me. Even though I was pinned to his bed, I was forced to look him in his eyes and what I saw there was concern for me. He wasn't trying to do something to me, he genuinely wanted to know me, everything about me. I wanted someone to know me. Why did I have to be alone in my nightmares? Samuel asked so many questions, he wanted all the horrible details and at first, I screamed, shouted and fought. But, he wouldn't let go, he held me there until he knew everything." I smile as I remember how childish we were. "Samuel saved me, pouring my heart out to him that night made me feel like I could breathe. Finally, the weight on my chest was lifted. Even now, if I'm having an anxiety or panic attack, just being in his arms calms me."

"There you go again," Shelly says pointedly.

I look at her confused, "What?"

"You get starry eyed when you talk about him, granted it's when you speak of him in the past tense, but it sounds like love." I knew what she was trying to say, I just didn't want to hear it. I stare at the ticking clock and notice it's ten minutes past five.

"I have to go Shelly; I plan to have dinner with Chase and his parents." I get up, gathering my things.

"Look Ariah, thank you for choosing me. I feel like I know you so much better, and my love for you has not changed. So, if you really love Chase the way you say you do, then let him in. Give him the choice to be your nightmare partner as well. Emotions are delicate things, especially yours."

"Tell me about it," I laugh to myself.

"Our minds and hearts can never come to an agreement sometimes, and that's okay. Go with your heart, go with your mind, it doesn't matter. That is my unbiased advice, however as your aunt, be careful, figure out what you want quickly. I know from personal experience what it's like to be strung along. Heartbroken people are not fun."

Falling onto my cushy couch feels so comfortable. I don't want to leave again, but I know how important this is to Chase. I put my dead phone on the charger turning it on. The first thing I see is a text from Chase canceling on me. I try calling him, but I get no answer. I lay back on the couch and decide to wait for him to call me back.

Even if my heart did want Samuel, logically speaking we would not work. Going against our parents is something neither of us can do. The feelings I had back when I wanted to enjoy the moment are no longer here. Why do I want to attach myself to Chase so badly? Before I could even introduce them, my father already decided our relationship was unsuitable.

I hate being afraid of what Chase will think, I like being on the pedestal he has me on. I liked being his perfect lady. If I tell him about my past, would all that change? If I were him, I would run. Nothing about me is perfect. I'm an emotional train wreck. Would he be able to handle it? I grab one of the cushions and stuff it over my face as I scream in frustration.

I stand up with determination, fuck this, why do I have to worry about this shit? I am Ariah Blackwood. Chase doesn't have a choice. He will love me because I love him. He will accept me because I accept him. If I must go against daddy for him, then I will. I can feel the adrenaline rushing through me. My new resolve has me feeling excited. I grab my phone and bag rushing out the door. I must see Chase, I have to tell him everything.

I jog to the frat house. I want to see him as soon as possible. Right now, nothing else matters, I choose Chase. I no longer want to love him, I just do. He has waited for me long enough. Walking up to his frat house, I notice there's a party going on. I walk into the house and the first person I see is Samuel, he does a light jog over to me.

"Woah, Ariah you can't be here." He stands in front of me, blocking my way.

"Where's Chase? No, you know what? I'd like to speak to you."

"Would you now? I thought you were afraid to be alone with me," he says with a smug smile.

"Not anymore." I look straight at him. Samuel takes my hand, walking us to the back of the house, we walk into the laundry room. Closing the door behind us, he stands in front of the door. Staring at his chest, I begin talking.

"I love Chase. I've thought this through long and hard. I've been holding myself back from him out of fear, but not anymore. The only reason I'm telling you this is because I want us to have closure." I look up, Samuel is staring at me, his face devoid of emotion. He's taking in everything I'm saying, like he always does. I look away. "I really want things to go well with him, I love who I am with him and how he makes me feel. I need you to let me go. I'm sure there's someone out there for you."

"You're still the same. I thought maybe you had changed. But no, here you are still being you." Samuel's jaw clenches. "You came here for what? Closure? What's that?" He's getting angry, so I try to walk past him. He grabs my arm, pushing me back to where I was standing. "I stood here and let you get all that off your chest, so now, it's my turn. You don't think long and hard about love, you just feel it. You know that already." He begins pacing. "I don't know why you keep running from me and I don't care. You and I are forever. You stand here telling me to let you go, I have said this before, if you want to make me the villain then fine, I'll be your villain. You left me, that is not very heroic. You were not the only one hurt by what happened. I lost a child that day too." I quickly blink the tears away.

"I blame myself for it every day. Yes, I was pathetic and scared. My father had just told me that I couldn't live the rest of my life with the love of my life. I thought, why keep doing this when we know the outcome? Then that night you sat there and talked to me. You believed in me enough to know that there was something wrong, that I wouldn't just cheat on you." Samuel stops pacing, he turns looking at me. "I have been looking for you all this time to apologize, to get on my knees and beg for your forgiveness." His eyes begin to water.

"Back then I was weak, childish, I didn't think I could fight them and win. I can stand here and say that I will make you love me, but I don't even have to because you already do. I know you better than you know yourself. You couldn't look me in the eye when said you loved him. Chase is not good enough for you."

Samuel pulls me into his arms, it feels good being here. Why did they think they could control me? My father and Samuel, both saying Chase isn't good enough for me. What about my feelings? Samuel's right, I don't love Chase, not the way I love him. But I can't trust him, he gave up on me, broke my heart, lost my trust and I lost my baby. I can forgive him, but I will never forget. I'll end up resenting him, always wondering when he'll dump me again. Or when he'll find the next skank to use and push me away. I don't want to live like that, and I don't have to. I'm a coward, but I'm doing the best I can to mend the broken pieces of myself. I push Samuel away, I can see the tears trying to escape his eyes.

"I don't want this." Samuel drops his arms from around me and backs away. I am not that sixteen-year-old girl anymore. I will not go backwards; I will move forward. I walk past Samuel and this time he lets me. I walk up to Chase's room and enter without knocking.

Chase is lying in bed on his back, looking up at his phone. He looks over at me and smiles, I feel my phone vibrate in my bag.

"Hey babe, I was just calling you." Ending the call, he sits up. Tears start falling down my face. I truly feel like I made the right decision. Seeing me like this is shocking to him, he jumps up and hugs me. I pull away from him and look into his eyes.

"What's wrong? You're scaring me. Did someone say something?" Chase cups both my cheeks in his hands. I move my hands to grab his.

"Nothing, I'm sorry." I try my best to calm down. "I don't know where those tears just came from. I missed you so I came straight over to see you," I say laughing it off.

"Yeah, sorry about cancelling. My parents had something come up. Plus, when I came back from class this shit was happening. The guys are having an impromptu party." Taking my hand, he leads me to his bed. "Look I don't know what's going on, and I'm worried. How about you stay with me tonight? You can talk to me about anything, Ariah."

I don't respond, and he doesn't pressure me to. I take my pants off, then get into bed with him. I came with the intentions of telling him my newfound feelings, however, all my energy is drained. I curl up under the covers. Chase wraps his arms around me and I feel my body relax. I'll talk to him in the morning, tonight I just want to rest.

Opening my eyes, I wake up to an empty bed. Reaching for my phone, I notice a text from Chase explaining that he is punishing the underclassmen for having the party last night without his permission. I smile, tossing my phone to the side. Standing quickly, I head into the bathroom. After freshening up, I decide to go home. I should stay here and wait for Chase to return, but I don't want to run into Samuel. My luck is nonexistent. As I make my way down the stairs, the first person I see is Samuel. I try to walk past him quietly, but he grabs my arm stopping me in place.

"I get it, you don't want to be with me. But not him, Ariah, it cannot be him. Do you truly know him? Look he's--," I snatch my arm away.

"Fuck you Samuel, you don't get to tell me who I can let into my life, you don't have a fucking say. I don't want to hear anything you have to say about Chase. I choose him, get over it. For the first time in your polished life, you can't have what you want." I turn to leave, but he pushes the door shut, trapping me in.

I can't move, I feel Samuel's body lean into mine. Taking a deep breath, I close my eyes. I can feel Samuel's breath on my neck as his fingers gently caress my hair. I can feel his lips brush against my ear, my knees buckle causing my body to lean into his. We stand in silence for a moment, neither of us saying a word. My heart is beating so hard and so fast. I'm trying to contain the excitement running through my body at his closeness. Before I can protest or move, Samuel grabs the back of my neck while putting his hand over my mouth.

"Shh, you have done enough talking. I can't have what I want, huh?" Samuel begins nibbling on my ear. "You should see yourself; see what you look like right now." His thumb caresses my neck. "If I can't have you, why are you reacting this way to me? Ariah, admit it, you belong to me." He lets me go and walks away without another word.

I immediately open the door and walk out. I can feel my face burning and my body tingling from his touch. I see Chase approaching with his underclassmen in a straight line behind him covered in dirt. Without thinking, I run up to him, kissing him as if my life depends on it. I hear shouts and whistles, but I ignore them.

"Shit babe, what was that for?" he looks down at me with lust in his eyes.

"For being you, I'm going to head home. Maybe we can hang out later."

"No can do, you see, my mom called earlier and said she would love to meet my beautiful girlfriend tonight. I, of course, told her that I would have to check and see if she's busy."

"No, I'm not busy, in fact I'm as free as the air I breathe."

"Good, pick you up at 6," he places a soft kiss against my lips.

Once I arrive home, I take a long hot shower. I lay on my bed in nothing but my towel. I begin feeling nervous about meeting Chase's parents. I don't like the fact that he has not warned them about me being black. Sure, I could be overreacting, but like I said, I've been through something similar before.

Picking myself up off the bed, I lotion and put on the best sweetheart outfit I can find. I hope Chase's parents like me, I will try my best to be likable. Thinking back, I wonder what Samuel was trying to say, I cut him off before he could finish. Knowing him, he was probably about to fabricate a story anyway. As I finish applying perfume, I hear a knock at the door, I grab my purse as I walk out.

Chapter Eight

The drive to Chase's parents' house is for the most part quiet. Looking over at Chase, I can tell he's deep in thought about something. I don't want to bother him, so I just look out the window. I still need to talk with him about so much, especially me leaving school. Every time I see his smiling face, I just want to forget everything. I have done so much talking this week that my jaws are starting to hurt. I reach over and grab his hand.

"Babe, are you nervous?" he asks, finally speaking.

"Yes."

"Don't be, I love you so I know my parents will. You are amazingly beautiful; you are the smartest person I know. You are too good for me, if anything they may feel bad that you have to be with me." I smile at his words. "Yes, she smiles! Stop worrying, if anything and I mean anything makes you uncomfortable, just let me know and we can leave." I don't respond. Sure, he says that now. I want his words to be true, but I know all too well what it's like to be loyal to your parents, not being able to go against them even if you want to. I look down at my hand holding his, this is something I will fight the great Charles Blackwood for. I don't care what anyone says, I will have Chase. We pull up to a restaurant, I look over at Chase with a puzzled expression.

"I'm not going in there looking like this. You should have told me we were coming here, I would have dressed appropriately," I huff, folding my arms. I'm sure I look like a child, but I don't care.

"Ariah, you look perfect, you are perfect. I want you to feel comfortable when meeting them. I get it, you're nervous, imagine how I feel. This is the first time I'm introducing someone to my parents. So, I'm trying to stay calm as well. I want you to like them and I want them to like you." Chase grabs my hand and kisses it. "My relationship with you is something I want for an exceptionally long time. This is serious for me; I hope you understand."

"So, I'm the first girl you've brought home?" I smile.

"That's all you got from what I just said to you?" He releases my hand. Caressing his face, I speak honestly.

"I'm in this for the long haul as well." Walking into the restaurant, my mind is more focused on not tripping over my feet. On the outside I am sure I look confident. With a model walk, courtesy of Shelly, I strut by the many people having dinner. This is the Blackwood way, we have a part to play, and we play it well. No matter what we're going through, we will look unfazed, in control and unmoved. My father once said, "people can smell fear on you, I'm not raising a scared bitch." We finally stop in front of a table where a nice-looking older couple stands and hugs Chase with open affection.

"Oh sweetie, I'm so happy to see you," the older woman says, hugging him tightly.

"Mom, don't embarrass me," Chase says, pulling away.

"Son, your mother couldn't possibly do any more damage than you've done to yourself," the older man says jokingly.

"Dad, it's good to see you as well." During their exchange, Chase's mother stares at me silently. I stare back, not because I feel challenged, but because I can see the surprise on her face. I awkwardly stick my hand out.

"Hi, I'm Ariah Blackwood." She pushes my hand away and hugs me.

"Wow! You are beautiful. Here I thought my son would have shit taste," she says, letting me go. "Please join us, you can call me Margo, it's been a while since we've seen Chase and I would love to hear how you guys met." Chase pulls my chair out for me, and I thank him. His father is quiet, while his mother does most, if not all, the talking. I'm curious as to why he's so quiet.

"Mr. Marano, Chase tells me you produce movies." This makes Chase and his mother look at me. I'm sure Chase is surprised at me for speaking up. Usually, when I'm around him, I'm his quiet little lamb.

"I dabble in the business," he answers, barely giving me a glance. I should stop here, but I decide to prod him a bit more.

"I was just trying to make conversation." I give him a fake smile.

He puts his fork down. "I'm just a little surprised. On the phone my son described you differently."

"Different how, if you don't mind me asking?" Before he can answer, Chase tries to interject, but his father shoots him a look that shuts him right up.

"Just different. I was sure a young naive girl would walk through the door on my son's arm, but you my dear, are not that." Mr. Marano takes a sip of his drink.

"No sir, I can assure you that I'm far from naive; my father didn't raise me to be." This man is pissing me off. I don't want to come off as aggressive, but his negativity is rubbing me the wrong way.

"Your father, and what exactly does he do?" This question makes Chase focus on me, since he and I only briefly spoke about our parents. Sure, I didn't want Chase to know who I am, but in no shape or form am I ashamed of letting the world know who my father is. I stare directly at Chase.

"My father is Charles Blackwood. He is the CEO of Blackwood Inc." Chase doesn't say a word as he looks at me. I can't tell if he is shocked or not, so I turn my attention back to his father.

"A businessman you say, no need to be modest, any person that knows money, knows your father. However, it does look like my son did not know this fact."

"We only briefly spoke about what our parents do. Besides, I don't think it's that big of a deal." I awkwardly glance over at Chase. He is still looking at me. His face gives nothing away, so I can't get a clear read on what's going on in his mind.

"Father, leave my girl alone. I brought her here because I wanted to give you guys a glance at what your future grandchildren would look like." This makes both his parents laugh.

"Hopefully, they take after you, Ariah," Margo says, grabbing my hand. I smile at her, but it feels forced. I hadn't thought that far ahead into our future, yet here he is talking about children. I must talk to him; I need to tell him everything. This man is sitting here seriously placing me in his future, how can I not choose him? Chase's parents are decent people. I can tell that they love their son very much. I can see myself going back and forth with his father over many small things in the future. I fit here, the four of us sitting at this table laughing and talking feels good. I want this.

The drive home is quiet. I want to ask Chase what he is thinking but I am afraid of his answer. I'm not this weak. What's wrong with me? As soon as I muster the courage to speak, my phone starts ringing. Looking over at Chase, I grab my phone. He doesn't spare me a glance.

"Hey daddy."

"Don't hey daddy me, have that fucker bring you home. I'm here waiting for you." I want to say no, but I just say what I always say.

"Yes daddy." He hangs up abruptly. I look at Chase, he's still deep in thought. "Hey, do you mind taking me home? My father is gracing me with his presence."

He looks at me with wide, curious eyes.

"Oh shit! Am I about to get the chance to meet the great Charles Blackwood?" After the day we've had, I don't want to ruin it. I know for sure seeing Chase is gonna piss my father off.

"Babe, he's not in a good mood right now. How about tomorrow we do lunch?"

"Don't tell me your father doesn't know about me. Wait, he does know I'm white, right?" I begin laughing.

"My father knows about you, and yes he knows you're white. I don't hide things from my father, not that I could." I mumble that last part. "His mood is sucky right now and I don't want to ambush him with my wonderful boyfriend." I give him my cheesiest smile, hoping that will be enough to convince him not come up with me.

We pull up to my building, and he leans over and kisses me softly.

"You did great today. Thank you for being you." I don't know what to say, his words echo in my head, and I know I should be flattered, but I feel like I'm only pretending. Would he still feel this way after he knows the real me? I get out the car. Before I close the door, I turn to face him.

"Chase." He looks at me. "I love you." I don't wait for him to say it back.

As I get on the elevator, I feel like shit. I just lied to Chase and myself. Walking down the hall to my door, I brace myself. I don't know why he's here or what I've done to upset him. My father, in all his glory, is sitting on my couch comfortably, texting away on his phone.

"Daddy, what brings you here?" He doesn't look away from his phone nor does he answer my question. I walk over and plop myself down next to him. The best place in the world is still right next to my father. I feel invincible, as if nothing or no one can hurt me. Finally putting his phone down, he pushes me away.

"You went to meet that piece of shit's family? I thought I told you he wasn't good enough for you?"

"You don't even know him, so how can you know his worth?"

"Ariah, I know enough. I'm not giving in on this, I've let you play around enough. I didn't think you were this serious about that fucker. I should kill his ass." I say nothing. "It seems to me that you and Shelly have been away from me for too long, I've come to get the both of you. We're going home as a family in two days. I just have to finish some business."

I gaze at his back as he stands heading to my door. I try to speak as calmly as I can. "Daddy, I am not a child."

Grabbing his coat, he gives me a hard look. I lift my chin in defiance, as I inwardly tell myself not to show any weakness.

"If you would stop acting like a child, I wouldn't treat you like a child. I was going easy on you by letting you come here in the first place. Do you think I'm about to let another one of these assholes that you think you love cause you to run away from me again? If it were not for John, Samuel would've been dead a long time ago." I stare at him in disbelief. "What, you thought I didn't know?" He walks over to the door. "Whether you or Shelly like it or not, I love you both and I love hard."

Of course, he knew, I wipe the tears from my face. Why did I think for a second that he didn't? My father is a man with many talents, he knows how to make an entrance and now I have learned firsthand that he can make a killer exit. How disappointed it must have made him to know his only child had gotten pregnant as a teen and miscarried? He never showed his disappointment, he only ever treated me as his little girl.

When I asked to leave for college, he never questioned it, he let me go. My whole life I knew I would end up doing one thing, following in my father's footsteps. So, I made no other plans. When I was younger, I told him of my dream and here he was making it a reality. Being like my father was not hard, studying and listening were easy, it was the heartlessness of it all. Unlike him, I'm weak. My emotional baggage is my weakness. He knows this, which is why he keeps me so close to him, why he keeps forcing me to be stronger.

I feel like I'm suffocating. I need to get out of this apartment. Stepping outside of my apartment building, I decide to go for a walk. I walk fearlessly through the streets. After all, I have nothing to fear. I'm sure there are four men following me for my protection. All these years I had tricked myself into believing I'd been living a normal college student life. Yet every day I had an entourage. I am never alone. They are always watching and reporting everything to my father. A hysterical laugh bursts from my throat, I don't want to accept it, but I know that I'll be leaving with my father.

I have never gone against him. I talk a good game when it comes to Chase, but I know our relationship won't last. The day my father let me know he wasn't good enough;

I knew being with him was impossible. This must be how Samuel felt when John told him the same thing about me. I can understand him, after all, we are our father's children. I look around, surprised to find that I have wandered to the front of the frat house.

Walking in, the first thing I notice is that it's quiet, too quiet. I shrug, the guys must be out. I decide to head to Chase's room, since I don't want to be at home. As I walk up to his room, I hear the distinct sounds of moaning. Why would a moaning bitch be in Chase's room? Before I can get to the door, I am pulled back and forced into another room.

"Why would you do that to yourself?"

"Fuck that, Samuel! I want to see for myself, that's the only way I'll believe it." I try to walk around him.

"Please, Ari, why don't you ever fucking listen? Why do you always have to learn the hard way? Just go home."

I look at Samuel in disbelief. "Is this what you've been trying to tell me all this time? Is this why my father is taking me back home?" It's all starting to make sense.

"I didn't know about your father, but yes, this is what I've been trying to tell you." He grabs my shoulders. "He doesn't deserve you and it sucks that you have to find out like this."

"And you do?" I pull away from him. Samuel stares at me in silence. I walk past him, all these men in my life have me fucked up. Sure, if they would have told me I wouldn't have believed them, but I would have listened, maybe not to Sam, but I would have listened to my father.

Bursting through Chase's door, I see him naked in bed with the bitch I fought outside last week. Everything is making sense now; this is why she tried to fight me. How long has this been happening? Why is this happening to me? I have so many questions, but I only need the answer to one. By now, we have an audience. It seems everyone knew what was going on except me. This makes me laugh, I'm sure I look crazy, but I don't care. I refuse to cry; he doesn't deserve my tears.

Chase jumps up and starts talking. I can't hear a word he's saying, because there's a storm swirling around in my head. I take a deep breath because I feel like I'm about to explode. There's one question lingering in my head. I watch as he manages to slip on his shorts. I notice that his slut is still naked on his bed, the same bed that I've slept on multiple times. Chase has her disgusting lipstick smeared on his lips, the same lips that I've kissed. I can see teeth marks on his shoulders, the same shoulders that I clung to in the past. I must look really fucking stupid. I feel really, fucking stupid. I want to leave and forget all this, but I still have this same question in my head.

"Chase." He stops talking while looking at me. I know there are people around and I may seem weak when I ask but I must know. I'll go crazy if I don't ask. I look him dead in his eyes, holding back tears,

"Was I not enough?" He doesn't say anything, he drops his head, staring at the floor. I take that as my cue to leave. As I'm walking out the door, I turn back. "Don't call me, Blackwood's don't give second chances." I walk out the frat house to find Ryan standing with the car door open.

"Miss, I thought you'd like a ride instead of walking." I don't respond as I step into the car.

Walking into my apartment, I kick off my shoes and head to the shower. After my shower, I crawl into bed and close my eyes. So much happened today, meeting Chase's parents and feeling a sense of belonging, only to return home to my father's forceful proclamation. Then finding out someone you want to love so badly doesn't love you at all. I feel betrayed, foolish.

Chapter Nine

When I open my eyes the next day, all the events of the day before comes rushing back. Looking at my phone, I realize I've slept the day away. There's no point in going to class today. I don't need to pack so I will just stay right here in bed. Thirty minutes go by, and I'm still in the same spot. For some strange reason, I begin wondering about my mother. What kind of life is she living now? Is she alive? Being sad makes me think about sad things.

I hear a knock at my door, I don't ask who it is, I already know. I open the door, and he walks in. I begin making my way back to my room, he grabs my hand and pulls me towards him. Before I have a grasp on things, I find myself crying like a crazy person in his arms. I'm unsure what I'm crying about, why am I so hurt? I'm tired of holding it in, being in his arms makes me feel like it's okay to cry.

It takes ten minutes for me to get myself together, finally he lets me go. My back was to his chest this whole time, so I turn and look up at him. Placing my hand on his cheek, I reach up and wipe away the single tear that's running down his beautiful face. He looks like he wants to tell me he's sorry, as if he knows the crime he committed against me was the start of all this. No matter what, I will never forgive him. Looking in his eyes, letting my tears run free, makes me want to cry harder. I'm broken, and all he has done is add more cracks.

We stare at each other silently, allowing our tears to freely flow. This isn't us though. Why is he standing in front of me so vulnerable, so defeated? Why are all these emotions hitting me at once, right in front of him? I know the answer, Samuel is my best friend, my only friend. Just like all those years ago, I want to pour everything onto him. I have missed him so much. Why is he always here to see me at my worst? He sees the ugly me, my ugly truth. Yet, I never feel judged. I never fear him knowing something about me. No matter what it is, he will hold me hostage until I tell him everything. I laugh at the thought.

"I meant it when I said that Blackwoods don't give second chances."

Samuel pulls me closer to him. "I'm not here for a second chance, I'm here for the continuation of our relationship. When you left, that was you running away from me, this," he points between the two of us, "is forever. Chances do not exist here, you and I, we just are."

Samuel has always had a way with words. He knows what to say and when to say it. I know he means every word; he and I will always be right here, never moving forward, stuck in limbo, because of our parents. I know this sad truth and so does he. I know how to maneuver through everything else life throws at me, but not this. Why can't I walk away? Why can't I tell Samuel to leave? What's stopping me from telling him that I don't want this?

I scream in frustration as Samuel watches me. I'm having a war with myself; I am always at war with myself when it comes to him. But then, I do something even more insane. It's like my body has become tired of waiting and made the decision on its own. I kiss Samuel, hard, something I have been wanting to do since I saw him on that porch. My whole body ignites, waves of energy run through me. I can't contain my emotions, and truthfully, I don't want to.

Our tongues are in a fight and as always, he is winning. I once asked him why he was such a good kisser, and did he kiss other girls the way that he kissed me. Samuel looked at me and said, "only you, because I kiss you with all my heart." He had said this to me with a straight face. I didn't laugh at how cheesy he was because I knew he was telling me the truth. Every time he kissed me it was rough, passionate and demanding, just like his heart.

I never understood what he meant when he said that to me until right at this moment. I relive all the memories with him, even the ones that are hurtful, I put them all into the kiss. I'm trying to convey everything to him through this one kiss. Samuel's hands are all over me, while mine are tangled up in his hair. He moves his hands down my shirt, pulling it over my head, leaving me only in my underwear. I immediately attack his lips again, sucking on them as I gently bite down. I smile as a soft moan escapes his lips. Picking me up, he pushes us up against my hallway wall.

Holding me up against the wall, he stops kissing me. In the silence, our breathing is labored and audible. I can't find any words to say to him nor can I catch my breath. With Chase I had all these intimacy issues, I didn't like hugging or kissing, but with Samuel, I can't keep my lips and hands off him. I pull his shirt off and begin kissing his neck. In the past, I never did this because we thought we were hiding things from my father and John. I want to mark him as mine, just as he believes I belong to him. Stopping to look at my handiwork, I smile.

One minute Samuel has me pinned against the wall, the next I am being tossed on my bed. He looks down at me, admiration in his eyes. I watch as his eyes move from my face, down to my breast, my stomach then my legs. Licking his lips, he begins taking off his pants, laying on top of me he starts attacking my neck. Samuel's hands are rubbing up and down my thighs. We have done this so many times that he knows all the places on my body to touch and how to touch them.

Moving down further to my breast, he takes his time kissing each one. He is being so gentle that it's driving me crazy. His lips feel like light feathers are being rubbed softly across my breast sending chills through my body. Air gets caught in my throat and I hold my breath in anticipation as he moves down further, kissing all over my stomach.

Samuel makes it to his destination, then pauses to look up at me. "Deep breaths Ari, you know what I'm waiting for."

Without hesitation, I take a deep breath, "please Samuel." My hands grip the sheets, "take me to another world."

I feel his tongue slide up and down my panties. I'm breathing so hard it feels as if my heart will explode. He pauses, placing his thumb where my clit is, rubbing it around in a slow circular motion. I don't know if it's the fact that I still have my panties on, but it feels so good. While he's doing this, he bites down hard on my thigh. Feeling this pain and the gentle motion of his thumb at the same time is putting my body in a frenzy.

"Sammy," I cry out. I hear him chuckle.

"What's wrong, my sweet Ari? You want me to take your panties off?" He bites me again while speeding up his thumb's movements.

I arch my back pushing my body into his touch. "Yes please, Sammy, take," hard breathing, "them..." before I can even finish my sentence, I climax. I lay on the bed panting, trying to come down from this high.

"Ari, has it been that long? Did poor Chase not know how you like to travel?" I begin giggling.

"No Sammy, only you know how to pilot this ship." Samuel's hands are now on my panties pulling them down.

"Ari, it's been too long." Before I can even register his words, he begins his assault.

Samuel is slurping everything up, not letting anything touch the bed. I can feel my fingers cramping up because I'm gripping the sheets so tightly. How did I go so long without this feeling? I feel everything. I'm reaching that familiar high again. Giving my hands some relief, I grab his head. Rubbing on his head like a mad woman, I want to prolong this feeling. I can't help myself, he's hitting all the right spots at the right time. How could he know my body like this? It's like he's reading my mind. I feel myself about to release again.

"Sammy," I cry out. I climax again, my legs are trembling and Samuel is still licking away. "Please Sammy," this is all I can manage to say. Samuel begins kissing his way up my body, reaching my lips, he kisses me with all his heart.

Moving his hand down to my thigh, he pushes my knee up to my stomach. He stops kissing me and looks me in my eyes. I know what he's asking. I kiss him again. I bite his lips as I feel him slide inside me, the sensation causes me to moan loudly. It has been way too long. He's moving slowly, giving me time to adjust. I start sucking on his neck, which causes him to grunt, and then he abruptly stops, and flips me over.

He enters me again, this time I can feel him much deeper. Samuel is moving faster and harder. I feel like my face is melting into the bed, and with every stroke he's hitting that magical spot. I concentrate on that feeling, squeezing myself around him. The sound of our bodies moving together is exhilarating. Suddenly, I feel that amazing tingle again.

He pulls my hair, causing me to lift off the bed. My back is pressed firmly against his sweaty chest. His breath tickles my ear. Slowing down, he puts one hand on my lower back pushing me away as he grabs my neck pulling me back to him. Samuel speeds up once again, and I feel like my whole body is levitating off the bed. His grip around my neck tightens a little, making me even more aroused. I feel him everywhere, my heart, my head, my body and my soul. My stomach tightens up as I prepare to release again. I squeeze my eyes tight as I focus on this amazing feeling. Samuel bites my earlobe hard, and that's all I need to let go of it all.

Letting go of everything without holding back, I squeeze myself around him. His hand that was on my back is now wrapped around my stomach. He's holding me so tight that I'm sure I'll be bruised. My selfishness doesn't allow me to notice that he's releasing too. Samuel lets my body go, and I collapse onto the bed. I have no energy; my muscles are like jelly. Samuel gets out of bed and goes into the bathroom. I hear the faucet briefly, then the unmistakable sound of the bathtub being filled. Coming back into the bedroom, he picks me up and walks us into the bathroom. He places me gently into the tub, then gets in and sits in front of me. I reach for him, wrapping my arms around him, holding him close.

"I love you."

The words echo off the bathroom walls. It must be the after sex high we're coming down from. I know Samuel loves me, at least I believed he did once upon a time. We once agreed to never say those words to each other. We agreed to just let things be the way they were. Why did he just do this to me? He had talked about loving me in the past tense. But to say it clearly right now in front of me? I can't stop the tears from falling.

"Ariah, why are you crying?" Samuel asks, not moving a muscle.

"Samuel, you can't love me. We can't love each other." My quiet sobs are all that can be heard. What is he thinking?

"But we do," he says, forcing me to face reality. I close my eyes.

"I've been going to therapy, with Shelly. I told her everything, all of it. It felt good telling her about my mom and you. It felt like a huge rock had been lifted off my shoulder every time I left her office." I laugh to myself. "She kept insinuating that I'm in love with you because of how my eyes look when I talk about you." I look up at the ceiling, the reality of our situation weighs heavily on me. "I wanted to forget; I wanted all my feelings for you to just disappear. I didn't want you to exist in my head anymore."

The tears start falling again. "She's right, I was in love with you back then, and I'm in love with you now. I love you so much and so hard, that I can't allow myself to forgive you." Samuel listens quietly. "I feel like you gave up on me, you decided my feelings didn't matter when you started pushing me away. How could you do that to my already broken heart? How could you not know how important you are to me? I willingly let you in, I willingly gave you my heart. I know people are betrayed every day, but I never expected to be betrayed by you." I'm so tired of crying, but everything is coming down on me at once. "How is it that my love couldn't give you the courage to love me the way that I love you?"

Nothing else is said, we sit in the water, lost in our own thoughts. Samuel gets out the tub, turning the shower on he helps me out. I feel like everything I've wanted to say to him for the past two years, I let out in one week. We shower in silence. I stare at him, waiting for a response. Once we are finished, Samuel begins drying my body. Following his lead, I grab a towel, drying him off as well.

I notice a scar on his leg, it's a scar I've never seen before. I pause looking at it, "what happened here?"

I look up at him as he stares down at me. "A week after you disappeared, Charles came to my house. I was in my father's office. My father was telling me that he knew what happened. He said, *'if I know what happened between you and Ariah, then you know that he knows what happened too'*. When my father told me to leave you alone, he told me that if I didn't and Charles found out, there'd be nothing he could do to stop that mad man." I stop looking at him, without thinking, I begin caressing the long scar.

"When he stormed my father's office, my father just sat there. Charles pulled his gun and pointed it at my head. My father pulled his gun out and pointed it at Charles. I thought I was going to die; you know how your father is. My father's words stopped him, *"he is my son and I love him."* Funny enough, that was the first time I heard my father say he loved me. Charles looked at my father for a long time, then he put his gun away. Your father looked at me with tear filled eyes, it was at that moment I decided to give him whatever he wanted. If he wanted me dead, could you blame him? I impregnated his daughter, caused her to have a miscarriage, then became the reason she ran away from home."

"Charles walked over to my father's bar and poured himself a drink. He looked back at my father, *'John, he took something very important from me. He hurt her and I feel helpless because I can't do anything about it.'* They started having a full-blown conversation about my fate like I wasn't standing there. *'Charles, I can't let you kill him, he deserves it, but he's still mine.'"*

Listening to Samuel's story, I can imagine where it's going. My father and John have a relationship that I will never understand. I don't know what to say, so I just stay quiet.

" I knew I would have to suffer the consequences of my actions, that was something they both taught us. My father looked at me as he spoke, *'I'll do it, I'll take something from him'.* Charles said nothing and watched as my father pulled a machete out from under his desk. He walked over to me and pushed it into my leg. Pain like you wouldn't believe radiated through my body. I could tell from the look in his eyes, he didn't want to do it. I saw a tear fall down his face as he twisted the machete in my leg, making sure I could never play football again."

I know who my father is, I know who John is, so I am not surprised by this story. My father and John are both insane, I knew this from a young age. They have done worst things to better people. Back then, I didn't think about how it would affect my father; I just knew I needed to get away. Charles Blackwood is everything that everyone says he is, but to me he is my hero. A feeling of guilt attacks me, because back then I selfishly put my feelings first.

Once I'm in my pajamas, I crawl into bed. Samuel climbs in next to me. We lay facing each other.

"Does it still hurt?"

"No, before he pulled the machete out, they called the doctor. Both of them helped me to my room. The doctor got there and treated it quickly. I couldn't walk for a while and had to have physical therapy. But I healed; I couldn't play football anymore." I stare at him as his lips move. This is the only person in the world that knows everything about me.

"Samuel, tell me something I don't know about you." I want to change the subject, to pretend we're a boring normal couple who don't have to deal with extreme parents. Samuel stares at me, his face is blank, but I can tell he's contemplating if he should tell me something or not.

"When I was five, my mother committed suicide in front of me." I blink rapidly, did I hear him correctly? Why is this my first-time hearing of this? I have many questions, but I do my best to remain composed. "I thought my childhood was pretty normal. I had my mother who stayed at home, cooked, cleaned and took care of me. I had my father, who went to work every day and would always come home with flowers or a gift for my mother. My mother was always smiling, laughing and playing with me. She was incredibly beautiful and kind. At that age, when I knew nothing and she knew everything, I believed she was the smartest woman in the world. How could the five-year-old me know that my mother walking around the house with chains on both her ankles wasn't normal? We lived in a mansion, but I never questioned why my mother was only ever allowed on one side of the house. I was free to roam around and go outside, she was confined, literally, to the west wing of my father's house. My beautiful mother, chained to a wall all because John Conrad loved her."

I watch as his facial expression turns into a scowl. "She didn't want to be with him. He abducted her and held her prisoner for seven years. She had no family, no one to look for her. She was raped and forced to carry me. She tried her best to smile at me, to love and nurture me, but she could only lie to herself for so long. She had to look at me every day, a child she never wanted with a man she didn't choose." I struggle to find an appropriate response to his story.

"On the day she killed herself, she told me everything. She laid everything on a five-year-old. She told me that even though she had gone through so much with my father, she still loved me. My mother slit her own throat with a smile on her face. I remember my father coming home and destroying everything. He went into a rage, yelling *'how could you leave me, I fucking loved you'*. I remember looking at her dead body in a pool of blood. Her eyes were open and that smile still on her face. After a while, Charles came to get me. He yelled at my father for allowing me to sit there looking at her body. He took me to his house where Michelle hugged me all night."

"When I was 13, I finally found the courage to ask my father about everything. I wanted to know why my mother had been in chains. And if everything she told me that day was true. He looked right at me and said, '*Samantha was an unlucky woman because I loved her. I loved her so much that I couldn't be without her, and because she knew this, she left me the only way she could.*' I hated my father because of what he did to my mother. I promised myself then, that I would never force the person I loved to do anything."

Samuel turns on his back and stares at the ceiling. "It wasn't until I met you that I started to understand him. I saw myself becoming just like him. I love you, so I want your everything, even if you don't want to give it to me. When it comes to you, nothing I do makes sense." I rest my face against his neck as he pulls me against his body. Why do we have to go through so much? I know that when we wake up tomorrow, we won't be able to cry anymore, we'll have to leave all the tears and emotions here in my apartment. We are the damaged products of damaged people. There will never be a happy ending for the two of us.

"Samuel, I love you so much." I wrap my arms around him, trying to get as close as possible.

"I know Ariah, I love you too."

Chapter Ten

I wake up to the smell of bacon. I sigh, daddy must be here. I go into the bathroom and brush my teeth. Looking at myself in the mirror, nothing is different. I'm still beautiful, still smart, still confident, still tainted, and I am still a Blackwood. Samuel is nowhere to be found. I'm sure he left so he wouldn't have to see my father. I brush my wild, untamed hair to the back of my head putting it in a tight ponytail. I was so preoccupied last night that I forgot to wrap it.

I walk into my closet to find something appropriate for photographs. I'm traveling with my father, so I'm sure there will be photographers everywhere. Once I've chosen a proper outfit, I put my phone charger and laptop in my purse, grab my phone and sunglasses then walk into the kitchen. My father is sitting on my couch comfortably. I walk into my kitchen to see Samuel cooking breakfast.

Watching him confidently stand there while my father is in the other room makes me smile.

"Good morning, Samuel," I say with questioning eyes.

He looks at me and shrugs his shoulders, "Good morning, Ariah." I walk back into my living room and sit next to my father. He is on his phone, but still positions his arm for me to curl under.

"Do I not get a good morning, or are you still upset?"

"Daddy, are you aware that Samuel can't cook?" I ignore his question.

"Yes, he did mention it. However, in order for me not to kill him for trying to sneak out of my daughter's apartment, we made a deal." I start laughing.

"I could never stay mad at you, daddy. I just wish you would have told me." I begin playing with my fingernails.

He kisses my forehead. "Ariah, no matter how hard I am on you, I don't ever want to see you hurt."

"Somebody's become a softie," I sing playfully.

"I'm a father, what can I say? I'm a sucker for my daughter."

Just then Samuel walks in, "umm, breakfast for two is ready."

My father gets up and goes into the kitchen, I stand as well. Samuel grabs his coat, winks at me, then leaves. I go into the kitchen to have breakfast with my father, it isn't the best, however it isn't horrible. My father stares at his plate, I laugh at him as he complains about the eggs being runny. He grabs his phone and dials a number. I laugh when I hear him on the phone with John asking why his son can't make eggs. Poor Samuel, John is probably going to yell at him. After the breakfast fiasco, we head over to my aunt's place.

"Ariah, stay here I'll be back," my father says stepping out of the car. After about thirty minutes, I hear yelling coming from outside. I look out the window and I see my father carrying Shelly over his shoulder. I can hear her yelling at him to put her down. Ryan opens the door for my father, he sits her down then sternly looks at her, "Michelle, keep trying my patience."

I watch as Shelly's shoulders slump in defeat, she turns, placing both her legs into the car. My father puts her seat belt on, then closes the door. Shelly has a tear coming down her face and I can't help but laugh, she is acting like a child. Scenes like these happened a lot when I was growing up. One would think I was the aunt and she was my father's daughter.

"Shut up Ariah, this isn't fair! Why do I have to be ripped away from my life?" I don't respond; I feel like this is a conversation that has nothing do with me.

"I'm not ripping you from a life you built all by yourself, I'm ripping you from that imbecile Marquise." He grabs the rim of his nose and sigh in annoyance. "Michelle, he's a fucking drug dealer, have you lost your fucking mind?" The tension is stifling, but I don't move a muscle. I look in the rear-view mirror and my eyes meet Ryan's. I mouth the name "Marquise", and Ryan shrugs his shoulders. "You and Ariah have fucking lost it. Both of you make horrible decisions when it comes to men." Shots fired, why did I have to catch a stray? My aunt pushes my head back so she can get a better look at my father.

"Do I, Charles?" My father looks at her with a fury I've never seen before. She lets my head go, looking out the window.

"Shelly, I caught Chase sleeping with some whore," I say, trying to change the mood. She looks at me with a sorrowful expression. She quickly pulls me into her arms.

"I'm so sorry to hear that-", before she can finish, my father interrupts her.

"I told you he wasn't good enough, if the both of you would just listen," Shelly smacks her lips.

"Charles, you know what's good for everyone besides yourself. You would rather live miserably instead of being true to who you are and the things you want."

"This and that are two different things. I live the way I do for a reason. I don't live a life where I can make rash decisions or live on the edge."

"So, loving someone is a rash decision?" She looks at me. "If that's the case, then where does that leave Ariah?" There are a lot of things circling in the air that confuses me. How has my dad not been true to himself? I know him to be a man who gets everything he wants. He accepts 'no' from no one. Is my father in love with someone?

"Shells, these are separate things, stop comparing the two."

"No Charles, love is love, no matter who it's between. You just fear what Ariah may think or how she may react. That fear is doing more harm than you think. A family shouldn't have secrets."

"Dammit Michelle!" he yells. "I believe I've told you before not to involve me in your doctor bullshit. I don't want to talk about this anymore." He pulls his phone out, indicating the end of the conversation.

I quietly reflect on the conversation. Love? I've never seen my dad with anyone special over the years, but I hadn't really been paying attention. If I ask, I'm sure he would tell me. If he is in love with someone, why would he be ashamed? Could it be a man? Is he gay? I've only ever seen him with me, Shelly and John. Wait, is my father in love with John?

It would explain a lot. Why hadn't I noticed it before? When I was living with my father, I would be around him 24\7, except for when he went on business trips with John. My mind is seriously blown. All these years, I've been so caught up in myself that I didn't think about what my aunt and father were going through. I still don't know the reason why Shelly moved away all those years ago. Pulling up to the air strip, we all get out the car to head back home.

Walking into the Blackwood mansion brings back so many memories. I feel like that six-year-old girl all over again. Only this time when I walk in, I'm greeted, everyone knows who I am. I don't feel out of place, this is home. My father and Shelly are still upset with each other, so I head to my room. I don't want to be around when they start arguing again. Walking to where my room once was, I open the door noticing that the room has been gutted. I turn around, looking at a new maid who has been following me, her name tag reads Tabitha. Before I can say anything, she speaks up.

"Miss, Mr. Blackwood moved your room. He felt that since you're older now, you may want a more secluded space of your own."

I want to be angry, but I let it go. Why did she let me walk all the way up here if she knew this was no longer my room? I close the door and smile sweetly.

"Show me the way."

I follow Tabitha to another wing of the mansion where the guest rooms are. We walk through a beautiful archway with double doors at the end. Tabitha walks ahead of me, opening the doors. My father turned the entire wing into one room for me. It looks just like my apartment in California. It brings a smile to my face. I really loved my apartment. I watch as Tabitha listens to her earpiece intently, she looks over at me.

"Miss, Mr. Blackwood would like for you to be down for dinner in one hour." I nod my head, acknowledging her statement. Quickly, she turns, leaving my room.

I'm not sure I like her; she purposely wasted my time. Now I must think of a way to get her back. I feel the old me coming back. I don't know why she hit a nerve, but she did. I smile at my pettiness. For now, I'll shower and get ready for dinner.

When I walk into the dining room, my father and John are seated at the table talking. They sound like they're in a good mood.

"So, you picked a grown woman up and dragged her home like she was a child?" John asks my father, an amused look on his face.

"She refused to come willingly," my father answers, taking a sip of his scotch. I walk over to the table and our butler pulls my chair out.

"The second most beautiful girl in the world has decided to grace us with her presence. I have missed you, Ariah. How dare you disappear on me? Your father, I understand, but me? I thought we were better than that." Before my father can respond to what John just said, Shelly walks in, drawing all our attention.

"Not tonight Charles, can we please act like normal people and have a normal dinner? No hitting, no fighting and no business." She takes her seat across from me.

"John, this is not over," my father says, glaring.

"Never thought it was," John replies childishly. "The gorgeous Michelle, thank you for allowing my eyes to see your wonderful face again." I almost choke on my water; this is where Samuel gets his cheesiness from.

Over the course of dinner, I quietly watch as my father observes Shelly and John flirt. Is my father jealous? Occasionally, John includes him in the conversation, but they don't interact much. Usually when John flirts with Shelly, my father intervenes. Shelly's words must have really affected my father. I am not sure what's going on, but I do want my father to be happy. There is nothing my father can do to make me hate him. So what if he's gay? He is still my daddy, the man I look up to, the man I wish to emulate. This is the reality, my father is secretly in love with his best friend, my godfather, John.

A knock at my door jolts me from my sleep. I sit up and watch as Ryan places four large binders on my desk. I don't ask him anything and he doesn't offer an explanation. I stretch, getting out of bed, I head to my bathroom. I shower, brush my teeth, lotion, then get dressed for the day. After I feel presentable, I head to my father's office. I walk in without knocking. I notice my father has another desk in the corner of his office, right where I use to sit. I happily walk over to it and take a seat.

"Do you like it?" he asks, looking at his computer.

"Yes, this chair is comfortable."

"Good," he looks at me. "Ryan should have brought you the information on everyone who works for the company." The binders. "I'm giving you a week to memorize all the details. You'll start shadowing me at the office. Just for old times' sake I want you to look over the files I put on your desk," he nods to the files as his phone starts to ring.

I pick up one of the files and smile at the nostalgia of it all, going through each page one by one, seeing things I am far too familiar with. This is the life I took a break from, but it doesn't feel wrong being back. I am my father's heir. He and I both put a lot of work into making sure I'll be ready to take over his company. I was ready when I graduated high school, but I had to get away.

After looking over the file and pointing a few things out to my father I decide to go check on Shelly. Unlike me, she has the same room next door to my father's. I figure she would be in her room, probably still sulking. Without knocking, I walk in. Shelly is still in bed under the blankets. I jog towards her bed and jump on top of her.

"Seriously Ariah, don't you think you're too old for this?" I wrap my arms around her, hugging her tight.

"What are you saying? I'm never too old to cheer my sulking aunt up. Come on Dr. Blackwood, it's not that bad being back here. Besides, daddy missed us." I let her go and take a seat in the chair next to her bed. She sits up, still the most beautiful woman I've ever seen. I mean she just woke up and yet her face is glowing. Sometimes I want to hate her, then I look in the mirror and see we look very similar. The only difference is that my skin is just a little lighter. Blackwood genes in full effect. I often wonder what my grandparents looked like.

"You wouldn't understand even if I took the time to explain it to you."

"Explain what?"

Shelly looks at me, then sighs. "I know what Charles means to you. I would never try to change the way you see him. I left for a reason and I wasn't ready to come back."

"Then tell me why you left," I say, realizing that something serious is going on.

"It's too complicated."

"I am not a child Shelly; I can do complicated. If you want to be mad at daddy and act like a child, then fine." I stand, ready to leave. "You want me to open up and tell you everything that's going on with me, but then you leave me here in the dark. I don't know what's going on and I hate it. I love the both of you, and all these secrets are tearing us apart."

"If I sit here and tell you the man that your father is, or the woman that I am," she pauses," and it's horrific, could you still love us the same? Could you still give that speech? Ariah, it's true that there are things you don't know, but there will always be things you don't know. Just take this dispute that Charles and I are having as one of those things."

"No, I refuse. If I remember correctly, Blackwood's don't lie to each other and we don't keep secrets from one another." I walk out, slamming her door.

When I get to my room, I plop down on my bed. My father and Shelly are treating me like a child. So, my father is in love with John, what's the big deal? That won't make me love him any less. And what is she talking about when she said, "the man he is, the woman I am." I'm getting frustrated with her roundabout way of saying things. The only thing I can think to do to get my mind off things is memorize the information in these damn binders. We have a lot of employees. The pages in the binders are specific, every detail one might want to know about another person is included, even information regarding how each employee has contributed to our company.

Finally pulling my eyes away from the binder in my hand, I look at my phone. There are three missed calls and 5 text messages, all from Samuel. Ironically, he must stay in California. John says he must finish what he started. Since he transferred there, he needs to graduate there. Thinking about it, my reaction to seeing John was normal, you would think that after knowing what he did to Samuel's mother I would be at least a little wary of him, but I'm not.

I trust my father, so that means I trust John. My father told me he is the only other man in the world that I can trust. So far, that seems to be true. Taking a break, I call Samuel. I miss his voice.

"She blesses me with her voice," I blush.

"What are you doing?" Listening to myself I sound like a lovesick teen.

"Nothing much, I was called back to the east coast. My father wants me to learn how to make eggs. His exact words, 'my pride won't allow me to let you walk around this earth an idiot'." I can't help but laugh.

"John made you get on a plane, fly across the country, so he could teach you how to make eggs?"

"He taught me himself. I fly back out tomorrow. I want to see you before I leave. John is gone, so I'm all alone."

I look at my phone, it's only 6:15 pm, "Sure, I think I can arrange an impromptu meeting, plus you could help me memorize my employees."

"Ariah Blackwood is being thrown to the wolves so soon?"

"Next week."

"What should I wear, sexy casual or sexy nothing?" Samuel asks. I blush and giggle at his cheesiness.

"Sexy nothing, I have to have dinner first, then I'll be on my way."

"Ah yes, the Blackwood mansion rules."

"Bye Samuel," I sing out.

"Bye beautiful."

Sitting in my room, I can't stop the smile on my face. I have forty minutes left before dinner, so I'll shower, eat dinner and go to Samuel's and have dessert. I don't have to hide my relationship with him anymore, everyone knows. Plus, I don't want to hide it. I don't even know what I would call our relationship but like Samuel said, "we just are".

I skip down the stairs making my way to the dining room. Surprisingly, it's empty. Ever since I can remember, my father has always been the first person at the table. Instead of taking a seat, I walk to the kitchen to see if he's in there. Peeking my head through the door, I only see Tom barking orders at everyone, trying to make sure dinner is perfect. I make my way to his office. I know he hadn't left for an emergency or anything because I would have been notified.

Walking down the hallway towards his office, I hear what sounds like objects hitting the floor. Maybe a deal didn't go the way he planned, so he was letting off steam. Now it'll be my job to calm him down. I don't hear yelling though, which I count as a good sign. The door is slightly cracked. Instead of just walking in and possibly getting hit by something, I peek through the crack. The view that greets me has me frozen in place, like a dear caught in some fucking headlights.

My father, with his pants hanging around his waist unbuckled, is thrusting aggressively in and out of my aunt Shelly. Yes, my motherfucking aunt. Who by the way has her legs wrapped around him, hanging on for dear life. As I stand in the doorway in a daze at what I'm seeing, Shelly makes eye contact with me. Her gaze is filled with passion and desire. She isn't shocked or ashamed, she looks unfazed as she watches me watch her get drilled by my father, her brother. She closes her eyes and tosses her head back in ecstasy.

I take a step back hitting the hallway wall. The way she looked at me let me know that this was something she wanted me to see. I start to make my way back down to the dining room, stumbling on the way. I take a seat at the table to the left of my father's chair as I always have. My face is blank, no one would be able to tell that there's a storm brewing within me. I can't unsee what I just saw. This is what she was talking about earlier today. This was what they had been talking about the day we flew back.

My father and Shelly are lovers. Just thinking this line to myself is sending chills down my spine. What the fuck has been going on in the Blackwood mansion? How has this been happening without my knowledge? Everything Shelly said and the way she said it, is starting to make sense. I'm so deep in my thoughts, I don't realize my father has taken his seat at the head of the table.

"So, how's the studying coming along?" he asks. Looking at him, he doesn't look like a man whose just finished fucking his sister.

"It's coming along. I have one more binder to look over, then I'll review all of them again." My father nods, looking down at his phone.

Shelly walks into the dining room looking refreshed. She looks like a woman in love. No wonder she always has a glow about her whenever my father is around. This shit is literally fucking me up. She looks right at me, still smiling.

"Ariah, your father and I have made up. We talked about it, I'm just going to open my practice here," she says looking me dead in my eyes. Shelly wants a reaction out of me. It's as if she's saying, 'I told you so'. Well, I won't give her the satisfaction. I need to organize my thoughts before I say anything about what I saw.

Putting on the best smile I can muster, "good, so no more arguing?"

Throughout dinner I can feel her watching me. I do my best to look normal on the outside, but mentally I'm falling apart. If I hadn't seen this with my own two eyes, I wouldn't be able to believe it were true. Shelly made sure I saw everything, she made sure I knew. Here I am, believing my father to be gay and in love with John. I was wrong as hell.

Once dinner is finished, I get up immediately and walk straight to the door. Out of the corner of my eye, I see Ryan scrambling about trying to get a team together to follow me. I don't care about that right now. I just need to get out of this godforsaken house. There is only one place I want to be right now. Getting into the car, I peel off not caring about the speed limit. Once I get to my destination, I don't even knock, I walk right into the house. Making my way up to Samuel's room, I hear the shower running. I go into the bathroom, peeling off my clothes I get in behind him, hugging him as tightly as I can.

"Ariah baby, what's wrong?" he turns facing me. He hugs me while kissing my forehead.

"Samuel, it's fucked up, really fucked up."

Chapter Eleven

I look up at Samuel, his eyes are shifting back and forth between mine, he is trying to read me. I take a deep breath. A small laugh escapes my mouth, and before I know it, I'm laughing hysterically. Samuel watches me cautiously. He couldn't even begin to imagine the kind of shit show is happening in my life right now. He turns the shower off, steps out and I follow. Walking into his closet, he comes out with a shirt for me, I throw it over my head then crawl into his bed. I lean my head back against his headboard, it has been a long time since I've been in this room. Samuel sits in front of me.

"Ariah, tell me something or I'm going to have you checked into a mental hospital." I say nothing. He moves closer, why must he always force things out of me? Before he gets too close and I lose my shit, I speak.

"Ok, fuck Samuel."

"Language."

I scoff, "I'm grown Samuel, I can speak how I want."

"Did you come here to argue?"

"No," I look away from him, folding my arms.

"Ariah?"

"Samuel?" He's getting on my nerves. As usual he's rushing me, but I need a minute. He gently caresses my leg.

"Samuel, I did have intentions of doing this, but things have now changed."

"Things, what things?" Somehow, he has managed to put himself in between my legs, he begins kissing up my legs. Almost losing my focus, I just blurt it out.

"Charles and Michelle Blackwood are fucking, and before you ask me if I'm crazy, I saw that shit with my own fucking eyes." Samuel bites into my leg leaving teeth marks. I wince slightly at the pain.

"Ariah, watch how you speak," he says rolling over on his back, realizing this is no longer sexy time.

"I know," I sigh in frustration." Fuc-, messed up, right?" I lay my head back against the headboard. "These past couple of days I thought my father was in love with John." Samuel props himself up on his elbow, looking at me. "Yes, Shelly and daddy were having an argument, she let it slip that he loved someone. Love and Charles Blackwood don't mix, so I started thinking, who is he with all the time? Why did he always get annoyed and hit John when he flirted with Shelly? Who does he call the moment anything happens? These were the things that pointed to him loving John, or so I thought." He is still silent.

"I was warming up to the idea of him being gay, I had a speech and everything. I was ready for him to come out to me." I thought I would be prepared for whatever my father threw at me. I start hitting my head against the headboard as images of him and Shelly pop into my head. While I am deep in thought, Samuel puts his hand at the back of my head to stop me from hitting it.

"How did you forgive John for what he did to your mother?" He pulls me down towards him, laying my head on his chest.

"Forgive? Ariah, you know we were not raised to have such traits. Forgiveness, I have no idea how that works." He has a point. John nor my father are forgiving people. They are vicious, petty and vindictive. They only know how to get revenge, an eye for an eye. Maybe that's why I will never forgive Samuel or my mother for that matter. "I had to accept that my father is a lunatic. I had to accept that he is a man who gets what he wants at any cost. I had to accept that he would not lie to me about anything I asked. He could've just told me that my mother was lying, that he would never do something as crazy as abduct a woman, marry her, rape her, then force her to have his baby. I just had to accept it. I used to wonder what my life would be like if I had never asked him for the truth. Would our relationship be different? My father has been nothing but good to me, sure I've received punishments over the years, but those were the consequences of my actions." Samuel takes my hand and kisses it. "Born with a spoon so silver it shines for miles. I wish I could say he was a shitty father; it would be easier to hate him," he says kissing my forehead.

"My father is a man who looked me in the eye and told me his truth. There was no regret on his face, his conscience was clear. He doesn't see what he did to my mother as something wrong. How I feel about it has no effect on him, no matter what, to him I will always be his son. He is who he is, there's nothing that I can do to change him, I know this, so I accept it." As Samuel speaks, I think about my father. Why am I upset about this? It's taboo, yes. Something society will definitely frown upon. But I remember my aunt saying that he only cares about what I think. What do I think? How do I feel? I'm even more confused now. I have so many questions.

"Ariah, I can't tell you what to do in this situation. To be honest, I have no clue what to say. Just ask yourself, can you accept Charles and Michelle being lovers? Does it bother you? How does their romantic relationship affect you?" I take my time thinking before I answer.

"Somehow I feel betrayed. I feel like I was left in the dark. I have no right to feel this way, I know, but that's how my selfish heart feels. My father was my flawless protector."

"Is he not now?"

"I don't know, sleeping with your sister is a pretty big flaw."

"Huge," Samuel says sarcastically.

"Shut up, that's still my dad asshole." I kick the side of his thigh.

"Right, he is still your dad, and Michelle is still your aunt." Samuel is right, I think as I drift off to sleep.

Feeling Samuel's arms around me as I wake up, makes me smile. His light snores are a comfort to my ears. Not wanting to wake him, I gently move his arm from around my waist. I slowly roll out the bed making sure my feet hit the floor first. I tug his shirt around me and quickly slip my pants on. While attempting to sneak out, a loud voice I am all too familiar with scares the shit out of me.

"Who do we have sneaking out so early in the morning?" John says from behind me. I'm too embarrassed to turn around. "You must be the new girl, Lara." Hearing that hits a nerve, who the fuck is Lara? Why would she be sneaking out of Samuel's room? I turn around with a disgusted look on my face. John burst out laughing.

"Ariah." He walks up, putting his hand around my shoulder. "You look just like Michelle with that look on your face. I'm quite famished. Breakfast by Ariah it'll be."

After quickly cooking an English breakfast for John and Samuel, I rush out the house. It is so embarrassing getting caught, and John didn't make it any better. He made fun of me the whole time and even refused to help with the cooking. Father is waiting for sure, John probably called him the moment I left. I pull up to the Blackwood mansion, still in Samuel's shirt. I walk up to the door as my father is walking out. He has a smug look on his face.

"Well, what do we have here?" Lifting his phone up to my face, there is a picture of me standing over the stove cooking breakfast with a smile on my face. "This picture cost me fifty thousand dollars." I give him a confused look. "That asshole called me saying he had something he knew I would want, then had the fucking nerve to say he wouldn't tell me what it was unless I paid him first." He looks down at the picture again. With a smile on his face, he says, "it was worth it."

I can clearly see the change in my father. He's happy to have the both of us home, especially Shelly. When she left, he became harder on me. I recall that he was always moody, unless he was directly talking to me or John. Back then, I hadn't suspected a thing. I should have known something was going on.

"Go inside, I'll be back by your first day, something came up," he says getting into his car. There is a caravan following behind him.

Walking into my room, I fall onto my comfortable couch. I feel nervous being back in the mansion. This place has so many secrets.

"What would Charles Blackwood do?" I think out loud. I get up, heading towards Shelly's room. The only thing I can think to do is ask the questions I need answered. I softly knock on her door; I hear her faintly say come in.

When I walk in, Shelly is sitting on her couch looking like the socialite she is. Her long legs are crossed, barely covered by her cream-colored skirt that fits tightly around her waist. One button has been left undone on her fitted blouse. Sitting erect, she stares right at me. The smile on her face is mesmerizing, she looks happy. Gross, did they just have sex? I walk over, taking a seat across from her. I cross my legs just like hers, though I don't look as elegant as she does, I try.

I want to hurry and get this over with. I want this to be the first and last time we ever talk about this. Maybe if I have answers to all my questions, I can accept their relationship. Much like my father, she looks unbothered. I'm starting to understand what Samuel means.

"I've been doing some thin-," Shelly cuts me off.

"Ariah, I'm in the mood for a story, would you like to listen to it?" I remain quiet. She looks down at her diamond studded bracelet, one I remember helping my father pick out for her. "Before we were blessed with you, it was just me and my big brother Charly."

Today like any other day I walked home from school alone. I was not afraid, all I had to do was walk down one long street, and eventually I would see my house. My big brother Charly told me that if I walked down this one street, I would be alright. I have never had any trouble making it home on time, I could always trust Charly's words. As I walked down the street, I saw a group of boys standing on the sidewalk. They were spread out on the sidewalk making it hard for me to get by.

"Excuse me," I spoke as loudly as I could. One boy turned around and looked down at me.

"Walk around," he turned back around. I looked around him and the only way I could get by was if I walked in the street.

A different boy named Tim looked over and noticed me. "Turk, move nigga, that's Les' little sister, you know how that nigga is."

"Man fuck him, she betta walk around like the rest of these mothafuckas." Tim shoved Turk to the side.

"Go ahead and get home little Les." I started to walk past doing what Tim said. As I rushed by, Turk stuck his foot out, tripping me, trying to catch myself I put my hands out in front of me.

"Damn nigga," Tim helped me up. *"Now you know his trigger-happy ass gon' come round here tripping. Fuck, you trip her for?"* I looked down at my bruised hands, holding back tears.

"Like I said, fuck that nigga and fuck his sister. That nigga younger than all you niggas, but he got y'all out here acting like a babysitter. This ain't his fuckin block." I started getting scared. I didn't know what they were talking about, I just wanted to get home. I started speed walking down the street. When I was almost home, I suw Charly walking towards me.

"Shells, why are you so late? What took you so long?" he asked, trying to grab my hand. I didn't want him to see they were scraped up, so I snatched my hand away putting them in my pockets. Watching me do this, Charly took my hands into his, looking at them.

"How did this happen, Shelly? Did you fall over something?" He stared at me, daring me to lie. Even though he had never hurt me, when Charly got mad, he was very scary. I did not want him taking his anger out on me like mommy, so I always listened to him. Choking back tears, I got over my fear and told him what happened. Charly didn't say anything, he just took my hand and we started walking back in the direction of my school. I panicked, that mean boy was in this direction.

"I want to go home Charly, please let's just go home." My tears flowed endlessly. He stopped walking and looked at me.

"Michelle, wipe your face. Niggas round here know not to fuck with us. Every decision I make out here affects our safety. You want to be able to safely walk home from school, right?"

I nod my head, quickly wiping my face.

"Ok, then suck that soft shit up," he turned and started walking towards the group of boys. As we got closer, someone noticed us. The group turned, watching Charly. It got eerily quiet. Charly looked down at me, then looked back at the group.

"Which one?"

I looked Turk right in the eye. I knew that if I pointed him out, Charly would do something horrible to him. However, I didn't want to defy my brother, so I lifted my finger and pointed at Turk. Everybody backed away from him. They all knew what was about to happen. Charly stared at Turk; he didn't say anything, he just looked at him.

"Oh, shit Les, this yo peoples, I ain't even know," he tried to play it off as a joke, but he was the only one laughing.

"Whether you knew her or not, don't matter big dog. She got hurt because of some shit you did. So, an eye for an eye, you hurt her, I hurt you." Everything happened in slow motion, one-minute Charly was next to me, the next he was in front of Turk hitting him with something black in his hand.

"You hard, huh?" Turk fell to the ground. "You think tripping my little sister makes you hard? Bitch, answer me!" He kicked Turk in his head. All the other boys just stood there. Tim stood guard making sure nobody else interfered. When Charly felt satisfied, he got off Turk. "I could kill yo bitch ass out here in front of all these niggas and nobody would do shit." Charly unbuckled his belt and pants. "You want to put on a show? Ok nigga, let me make you a star." Charly started

peeing on Turk. I was disgusted, but everyone else just watched mutely. No one tried to stop my brother.

Charly zipped his pants back up, then turned around and made eye contact with each boy standing around. It was as if he was asking them if they had anything to say about what they had just witnessed. No one said anything, no one moved to help Turk up off the ground. Just moments ago, they were all laughing together as if they were friends, now everyone acted as if they didn't know him.

Charly turned and headed home, and I quickly followed. This is how it was, all I had was my big brother and all he had was me. When we got home, our mother was sprawled out motionless on the floor. Charly walked over to her and checked her pulse. I stood frozen and frightened as Charly stood up and stared down at her.

"Michelle, go upstairs and pack a bag."

"What, why? What's wrong with mommy?" Charly walked over to me.

"If we stay here, some people gon' take you and then we'll be separated. Do you want to be separated from me?" I shook my head no, forcing the hysterical scream back down my throat. "Pack a bag with some of your clothes and shit and let's go."

I ran up the stairs and started putting clothes into a bag. Luckily, I didn't have much. My mommy wasn't good to me or Charly, but she had been all we had. Charly was unfazed by the whole thing; I did not want to make him mad by asking questions. I quickly ran downstairs; Charly took my hand and just like that, we left our mother dead on the living room floor.

We ended up living in a small apartment. I didn't have to stop attending school. It was like my mother hadn't died, or like she had never been a part of our lives. I didn't have time to cry for her, not that Charly would allow it.

"We don't shed tears for mothafuckas that don't care about us, we are Blackwoods, you and me," he had told me. I never understood why he talked like that, but I listened to every word as if it were gospel.

After Charly's first year of high school, he transferred to some white school in the suburbs. That didn't stop him from being in the streets. He said that was how we were going to survive. He told me not to worry and that it was not something he would be doing forever. Charly paid some lady *to take me back and forth to school, while he took the bus. The uniform he wore was always clean and neatly pressed. He would leave the house an honor student and return home a thug.*

Charly was never friendly, he once told me, "anybody that's not family, is just a tool for me to use so that we can get ahead. You're my only family so fuck everybody else." I listened as he spoke, taking it in and changing myself to be that way too. Until one day Charly came home early, there was blood all over him and he was not alone.

"Shells, this crazy ass white boy saved my life today, thus earning him the right to be a part of our life." The strange boy in the same uniform as my brother started laughing.

"I don't want to be a part of your shitty life, look at this place. It's literally the same size as my closet." Charly shrugged.

"That's right mothafucka, look around, become a witness, watch how I get to the top. See where we're coming from and understand why no one, not even those entitled bitch ass rich kids, can get in my way." The stranger walked over to me with a charming smile, I backed away.

"Shells, it's ok, he family." Charly then walked back into his room.

"Hi little goddess, my name is John." I glared at John. That was the first time Charly referred to someone that wasn't me as family. I was jealous. Charly had never let anyone in that wasn't me, he was all I needed, and I wanted to be all he needed.

Years went by, Charly and John's relationship became stronger. He visited the house more often and even picked me up from school a few times. By the time I turned 16, I realized that I was in love with my brother. Charly and John were in college. Charly had officially quit his street career. He was now starting a company of his own. John decided to help him with the resources he had. His father was suffering from cancer and had planned to leave everything to him. One night, John came to our penthouse apartment excited about an idea he had.

"Hello, my beautiful Belle, is the beast around?" he asked as he burst through the door. I pointed next to me, Charly was lying on the couch with his feet in my lap.

"Charles, we should definitely go somewhere this weekend. Samantha is acting moody right now and I need to *blow off some fucking steam." Charly looked up from the book he was reading.*

"She's probably moody because you got her chained up. I don't get why you can't just like a bitch that like yo ass back."

"I get it, you lonely piece of shit. You don't know what love is, so until you experience this shit, leave me the fuck alone." Charly shook his head. "Now let's go fuck some strippers." John got up to leave. "I'll be back later to pick you up."

I was having a small panic attack at John's invitation. I had never seen Charly interact with a woman besides me, so the thought of him ever entertaining another woman had never crossed my mind. As John was about to walk out the door, he stopped and looked at me. The look on his face showed pity, I remember him mouthing 'sorry' to me as he walked out the door.

That night I barely said anything. I was at war with myself. My feelings were stifling. I had been doing the absolute best I could to contain them and keep them hidden from Charly. What was wrong with me? Why was I sitting across from my big brother on the verge of tears just because he may or may not be fucking strippers tonight? I couldn't just stay quiet in my agony, I had to know.

"Charly," he looked up at me. "Are you a virgin?"

He stared at me, looking as if he was trying to think of the right thing to say. Charly's hesitation was enough to let me know that the answer would surely break my heart. When? Where? Why? And most importantly, with whom? All these questions created small explosions in my brain. How could I have been so naïve, so stupid to think that there was a possibility my brother was saving himself for me? Even if I was saving myself for him.

My tears betrayed me. I thought Charly would rush over to me in shock and ask why I was crying. Instead, he just sat there, and stared. A sad realization hit me; my brother would never love me the way I loved him. Charly would never want me the way I wanted him. He would never feel a need for me the way I needed him.

In the beginning, when I first realized I was in love with him, I thought something was wrong with me. Maybe there was, maybe there still is, but at that moment nothing mattered. The intensity of my feelings was becoming unbearable, my whole world was falling apart around me. To see him sitting there, just staring at me made me wonder if he in fact, had known about my disgusting feelings. Did he know how obsessed I was with him? Did my feelings burden him? Charly stood, heading for the door. I chased after him and grabbed his arm.

"Please, don't go." Looking straight ahead, he hesitated. My grip on him grew tighter. The moment of hesitation gave me hope, so I turned him around and without thinking, kissed him as hard as I could. Forcefully, he pushed me away. We stood there looking into each other's eyes. I was desperate. I held my breath, hoping he would stay. But he turned away and walked out the door.

The same night I let my brother see my true feelings, he fucked a stripper and got her pregnant. I waited for him to come home for a week, but he never showed. On the seventh day I got fed up and went to the only place I knew he would be. I stood in front of John's house pacing back and forth for about ten minutes before he opened the door scaring the shit out of me.

"How long are you going to stand out here walking back and forth? Come in, before I have to kill one of my dumbass neighbors for calling the cops."

John led me to the kitchen where Samantha was cooking dinner with a chain attached to her ankle. I didn't have time to worry about John and his psychotic ridiculousness, I needed to see Charly. I had told John that he shouldn't make the chain a permanent thing, but did he ever listen? Besides, I didn't feel sorry for her, I knew John really loved her.

"Hello Samantha," I smiled at her. She was a beautiful woman, everything about her screamed innocence. She had big blue eyes and looking into them would always make me feel inferior. I always felt small in front of her, it was as if she knew all my dark dirty thoughts just by looking at me.

"Hi Shelly, I see you've finally come to get your brother," she smiled brightly at me. You wouldn't know she was being held captive until you saw the chain.

"Of course, she has. She never comes to visit us, there is only one reason the queen would ever grace us with her presence." I smacked my lips.

"John, cut the shit, where is he?" I was getting impatient. John didn't say anything, he looked away from me and gave Samantha a kiss on the cheek. John was very touchy when it came to her, he could never keep his hands to himself.

His love for her always made me jealous, it was a love I wanted for myself.

"What did you do to him?" John asked while taking a seat.

I didn't say anything, I only looked at John as he looked at me. It was as if two people who understood each other had come to an agreement. When he had come to us with the idea of kidnapping Samantha, I'd been all for it. Why couldn't he have the one he loved? Why couldn't he fight in every way possible to have her? As someone unable to love freely, I sympathized with him. If I could chain Charly up, I would. Then he would only have me and I would only have him.

"He's in his room." John stood, giving Samantha a hug from behind.

I took my time walking up the stairs. I knew what I was going to say to him when I saw him. I'd had a whole week to practice. Getting to his door, I didn't hesitate, I walked right in. Charly was sitting on the side of the bed with his face in his palms. Looking around the room, I could tell he was trying to bury himself in his work. Books, files and loose papers were tossed all over the room. He must have sensed my presence because he lifted his head, almost in slow motion.

"Charly, let's go home." I could hear the desperation in my voice. He stood up, not uttering a word. I took that as my answer. I turned and walked out the room. He followed me out the house and into the car.

The drive home was quiet, neither of us said a word. What was he thinking? Why didn't he say anything about the kiss? Was he trying to forget it, pretend it never happened? I wouldn't let him sweep my feelings under a rug. I could feel myself about to burst, I wanted to reach out and hold his hand, but I was afraid he would push me away. I had never been an insecure person, but I felt very unsure in this moment. Why couldn't he just love me?

Once we got home, he went into his room and I to mine. I showered, put my pajamas on and walked across the hall to his room. He was still in the shower, so I sat on his bed and waited for him. My heartbeat accelerated when I heard the shower turn off. I sat up straight, staring at the bathroom door. Charly walked out with only his pajama pants on. I felt a fire ignite within me; how could I possibly be normal? I had to say something before I attacked him again.

"Did you fuck a stripper?" I spoke quietly, looking at the floor.

"I did," he answered, leaning on his dresser across from me. I could tell he was trying to keep his distance.

"You're not just saying that to hurt me, right?" I looked up at him as a tear slid down my face.

"I would never just say something to hurt you." I looked down at my hands again.

"Is it really that wrong for me to love you? Are you really disgusted by me?" The silence was deafening. I looked up at him, his face was void of emotions. It was as if this conversation didn't matter to him. I felt myself chocking up, why was I the only one affected by us being in a room alone together? "What should I do, Charly? I can't change the way I feel, I've tried. Is my love that horrible?" I was sobbing controllably now. "How can I turn my feelings off? Tell me how and I'll do it. I love you so much. Loving you this much is driving me insane. I'm jealous of fucking John! Why can't you just only need me?"

"Maybe you're confu-," I cut him off.

"I'm not confused, I know myself. I'm not a fool. You don't think I already explored that option?" I raised my voice

as my annoyance grew. "There must be something twisted in my head. How could I feel this way about my brother? Why do I want to kiss him? Why do I get nervous whenever he touches me so innocently? Why do I hate his friend for taking his time, time that could be spent with me? I've gone through all these questions in my head thousands of times, and they always lead back to one answer." I closed my eyes taking deep breaths, my words weren't reaching him. I stood up, walking towards him.

Charly put both hands up, "Shells, please don't come near me."

Hearing him say this, made me stop in my tracks. His rejection felt like someone was repeatedly punching me in the stomach. I felt like I was suffocating, and he was my oxygen. Did he think I wanted to feel like this? If I could control the way I felt about him, I would. If I could, I would shut all my emotions off. But I couldn't. I had to have him and he had to have me.

"Don't do this to me, please, don't push me away," I pleaded with him.

"Shells, you're my baby sister. Is it because I'm all you know? Should we live apart for a while so you can get over this phase?"

"Phase?" I repeated in shock. "Are you serious right now?"

"Michelle, do you hear the things you're saying? You're standing in front of me telling me you love me romantically, me," he pointed to himself. "Your brother. I've taken care of you your whole life, I raised you." He took a couple of breaths. "Tell me, how can I help you?" He looked so defeated.

"Just love me back," I answered pitifully. "Why can't we just love each other, just accept me, because I don't know what else to do."

For the first time in my life, I saw Charly cry. Tears were streaming down his face. No matter what he said or did, if he didn't love me back, I would be hurt. My whole life my big brother had loved and protected me, yet here I was hurting him far more than any other person ever could. I was so selfish; I just couldn't stop. I knew that this was not a phase; I knew that my love would be looked upon as wrong. I knew that Charly may never love me back, but then what should I have done? I couldn't live life without Charly. I never wanted to be separated from him. But there we were, broken, a brokenness that could never be repaired again.

I looked up at him as he looked down at me. My beautiful Charly with his tear-stained face, my big brother who I was hopelessly in love with. I had no choice, no matter what, I had to have him, he had to be mine. Fuck the world and anyone who would have a problem with it. My feelings would remain unchanged, and he would love me just as I loved him.

"Should I just die, Charly?" It took him a moment before he registered what I said.

"Why would you say something like that?" He grabbed my arms tightly, while looking at me with an angry expression.

"It hurts so much loving by myself." The tears wouldn't stop. I pushed him away. "I don't want to live in a world where I can't love you and you can't love me." I got up, moving towards the balcony. Without hesitation, I had decided that I would die. It was over. I didn't want to be a part of a world where I couldn't have Charly. As my foot touched the banister, I was roughly pulled back. Charly's body broke my fall as I fell backwards.

"Why would you leave me, why would you leave me, why would you leave me?" He asked this question repeatedly, while hugging me tightly.

Staring up at the starless sky, I took a deep breath. "At least if I died, I wouldn't have to feel this pain. I wouldn't have to feel all this hurt from you rejecting me."

Charly loosened his grip, he turned me so that we were face to face. The look in his eyes had changed. I searched them trying to figure out what he was thinking. He leaned forward, kissing me passionately and everything around me evaporated. I forgot that I had just tried to commit suicide, I forgot that the person kissing me as if his life depended on it, was my big brother. At that moment, Charly was no longer just my big brother, but Charles Blackwood, my lover, my teacher, my protector and my best friend.

All my life I had believed that my father was the most manipulative person I knew, but I now know that's not the case. I sit quietly, going over everything I just heard. I can't help feeling bad for my father. Shelly is scary. I look at her as she straightens her already perfect skirt over her perfect legs.

"Do you regret it?" I ask, causing her to look at me and smile.

"How could I?" She has a faraway look as she stares at the wall behind me. "The one thing I wanted most in this world, I have. Nothing else matters to me. This horrible me, who manipulated the love my brother had for his sister, his only living relative, how could I? I regret nothing. I want this love, no matter the cost." Her eyes stare into mine. "Look at it this way, if my insecurities hadn't gotten the best of me, Charly wouldn't have gotten mad and slept with your mother. Then I wouldn't have you."

She smiles softly.

"When we first got the phone call about you, I was excited to meet you. Who was this child that had Charly's DNA and not mine? The moment I saw you any jealousy I thought I had vanished. You looked just like my mother, you looked just like Charles. You reminded me of everything I love, so how could I not love you?" Standing, she walks over to the window. "Sometimes I wish I had a fickle heart, but once I love something, I have to have it. This includes you, Ariah. I felt like you needed to know, not because I wanted to hurt you, but because I was beginning to hate myself for hiding it from you." Something is still bothering me.

"If this love was something you wanted, why did you leave?"

"I wonder which one of us is the therapist," she says, laughing to herself. "Do you know why I studied psychology?"

"No," I answer honestly.

"I wanted to figure out if there was really something wrong with me, if I am, in fact, sick. In all my research on myself, I found only that I'm a selfish, manipulative, spoiled brat. I have abandonment issues and I hate being alone. I realized that what I had done to Charles was wrong." She turns, looking at me. "I didn't give him the chance to make a choice. I manipulated him into loving or at least making me believe he loves me. Once this realization hit, I started to doubt his love for me. So, in order to make myself feel better, I requested something from him. Something that would keep us connected forever."

"What did you ask for?"

"Shelly, what the fuck did you just say to me?" Charly looked at me like I was crazy.

"I said, I want to have your baby." I looked straight at him as I spoke. I wanted him to know I was serious.

"No."

"What, why? I want a baby." I began sulking. Charly remained quiet. "Charly, why can't we have a baby? Why can't I be a parent too? I want a little person that I can call my own. I want to make that little person with you." I pause and stare at him. "Are you still ashamed of me? Do you really love me?"

"After all I've given you!" he yelled, slamming his hands hard against his desk. "Michelle, is it not enough?" I chuckled, the nerve of him. I turned to walk out of his office.

"As a matter of fact, no Charles, it's not enough. I want every fucking thing."

"After that conversation, I became disgusted with myself. Not for loving him, but for forcing him to love me. I wanted his whole heart, nothing less. I had to get away, so I told him I wanted to live apart for a while. I had to assure him that I wouldn't try to hurt myself. He didn't even try to keep me here. He didn't try to talk me out of leaving, so I thought things were over. Then I met Marquise. I decided to use him, so I could see if Charles really loved me."

I stare at my aunt in shock, she sounds like a super villain in a damn superhero movie.

"Has loving him the way you do been worth it?" Looking down at her bracelet, she smiles brightly.

"The answer is yes. If I had to go back in time to start over, I would do everything the same." She looks over at me. "I don't need you to understand your father and I, I just need you to accept it. You're the only other person we love and care for deeply. Don't hate him, if anyone is to blame, it's me."

Chapter Twelve

Stepping out of my car, the cold air immediately hits my cheeks. Like any other weekday, I make sure I show up an hour before everyone else. Working at the company is now routine. I do nothing else with my life besides work. The past year has been very uneventful, but this was the life I had been trained to live, the life I asked for. Walking into the building, my assistant Ron rushes towards me. Ron is perfect. I handpicked him myself.

"Morning Ms. Blackwood, the chairman has asked for you to see him in his office first thing. Then you have a morning meeting with Mr. Ashley about a new investment."

We begin walking toward the elevators. "New investment? I know you can do better than that, what does he want with my money?" Ron smirks to himself as we step into the elevator.

"He wants to buy his father out, he doesn't want to run the business when his father retires. It looks like he's going behind CEO Ashley's back trying to sell. However, for him to do that, he would have to own one hundred perc-," I cut him off.

"I get the gist of the situation, if he wants to hand Cross Holdings over to me, I'll take it. When did my father get back?"

We step off the elevator on the top floor. There are only two offices on this floor, the office on the left belongs to the company's chairman Charles Blackwood, while the office on the right belongs to the president, Ariah Blackwood. There is a desk outside of each office. Thomas, my father's secretary, has a desk to the left. He has been with my father since he started the company. Though I've met him many times, we've barely had any interactions. He is my father's shadow, seen, never heard.

On the right is Ron's desk. One year ago, when I started working officially, my father told me to get myself a secretary. He said I should hire a man because they are easier to control. Ron stood out the most, not only because he played college football and was huge, but because he was the only one who looked directly at me as he spoke. I felt like I would never have to question his words, my father calls it blind trust. On the other hand, if Ron ever betrayed me or the company, he would be taken care of thoroughly. I turn towards my father's office.

"He got back in last night and came straight here." Fuck, something must have happened, fuck. Before I get close enough to knock on the door, the double doors open.

"Oh, Ms. Blackwood, he's ready for you. Ron, you are not needed," Thomas says, stepping to the side so I can walk in. My father is sitting at his desk staring blankly at his computer screen.

"You asked to see me?" I take the seat across from him. He looks up at me.

"I did." He begins rubbing his chin as he looks me over. "Ariah, when was the last time you spoke to Samuel?" Puzzled, I answer honestly.

"It's been a couple of days, he's been pretty busy with his graduation coming up, and I've been busy with the company. Why do you ask?"

"Are you in love with him?"

"Dad," I look at him, confused.

"I asked you a question, Ariah," he says loudly. I can feel my irritation creeping in.

"Why should I have to tell you about my personal life when you yourself never tell me anything about yours?"

"Ariah, answer the fucking question. Why is it every time I ask you about that damn boy you get so fucking defensive? You're showing me exactly what you're thinking, it's weak."

"Samuel is my weakness, so I guess that means Shelly is yours?" My father stares at me as if he's restraining himself from hitting me. I've seen this look countless times over the past year. He tries to throw Samuel in my face so I can throw Shelly in his. This is how he raised me. If I get a hold of a person's weakness never let it go, it can always be used against them. My father and Shelly are still carrying on with their relationship, just like I am with Samuel. We haven't talked in a while, but that's how we are. Whenever we're ready, we always come back to each other. Samuel has things he needs to take care of and so do I.

"I didn't ask to see you to fight," he takes a deep breath. "You and Samuel can't be together. He isn't someone you have a future with. I need to make sure you understand this." I look away from him as he continues.

"Ariah, it cannot happen. Look at me and say that you understand."

I stand, ready to leave his office. This is the first time he's ever told me that I can't have something. Before I can get to the door, he calls my name. I stop walking, turn around and look at him. I do not want to throw a temper tantrum like a child, so I'm trying to stay as calm as possible.

"Samuel is getting married, Ariah. John has arranged for him to marry and he agreed to it." Taking a step back in disbelief, I replay his words in my head. I don't know how to respond. I don't want to respond.

"I have a morning meeting, thank you for telling me," I say, walking out his office.

I walk straight into my office and pull out my cellphone. I pull up Samuel's number, but I stop myself before I press call. Taking a seat, I lay my head on my desk. This was something I knew from the beginning; something I have been preparing myself for. So, why does it hurt so bad? Why am I so angry? Even though I want to call him and hear his voice, I'm not sure how I'll react.

I'm no longer a person who can act on a whim. Everything I do has to be part of a plan; I must see all outcomes. I can't help feeling that this is another childish test. That my entire life has been one big test administered by my father to make sure I am second to no one. I close my eyes, pushing all my thoughts away. I don't have time for this. I must focus my mind on the task of acquiring a company from a backstabbing idiot. There is a knock on my door.

"Ms. Blackwood, Mr. Ashley is here," Ron says walking in. "Here is your coffee, cream no sugar and your father has left. He asked that you take over all his duties and that Thomas will assist you with anything you need." I roll my eyes as I take a sip of my coffee. "Mr. Marano from the production company you just took over is on line one, he'd like to meet with you."

"Thank you, Ron, send Mr. Ashley in, sit in on this meeting and have Thomas take care of the phones. Tell Mr. Marano we can have lunch. I refuse to go the day without food again. I have a taste for Italian." I look down at my phone. "Tell Ryan to find out where Samuel is."

"Yes, Ms. Blackwood." Ron walks out of my office to take care of the many tasks I assigned. Moments later, he walks through my doors with Mr. Ashley on his heels.

I stand to shake the piece of shit's hand. "Mr. Ashley, what brings you all the way here from Cross Holdings?"

"Mr. Ashley is my father, you can call me Brandon." He continues to hold my hand. I pull my hand away, while forcing a smile. There is no way I'm calling him by his first name, he should be lucky I'm being cordial. How could he turn his back on family? His father has given him everything and this is how he repays him? I can't respect a man that would turn his back on family. I'm torn from my thoughts by his disgusting voice.

"I have decided to sell off my father's business, but meeting you is giving me second thoughts."

"Second thoughts?" I look at him, unfazed.

"Well, Ms. Ariah Blackwood, we elites hear about you all the time, but I never thought you would be this beautiful. I can't take my eyes off you. This is making me want to keep the business and put a bid in to make you mine." I smile, I glance over at Ron. Ron has gotten use to these ridiculous spoiled ass brats, they walk into my office and think just because I'm my father's daughter and not his son, that they can let all kinds of shit fly from their mouths. This is not the 1800's, I don't need to marry. If I did marry, it wouldn't be to a weak piece of shit like this. It baffles me how all these elite rich heirs turn out to be the same. How did Samuel and I make it? How did we survive?

"Ms. Blackwood, are you over there thinking about my proposal?" he smirks at me. I am now even more disgusted.

"I'm thinking about my girlfriend's pussy. You see, I was feasting on it all night and just began to have flashbacks. Ron, what time is lunch?"

"You'll have a late lunch today, two pm." The look on Brandon's face is priceless. "Now, what was it you wanted to discuss?"

The day is going by slowly, luckily, I am so busy that I don't have time to think about Samuel. My father did this to me on purpose, another fucking test. Trying to break me early in the morning knowing he was going to lay a day full of shit on top of my head. I have no choice but to face his shit head on. I don't have the luxury of shedding tears, that'll have to wait. Half the day is gone before finally I get to eat. Hopefully, the company doesn't ruin my appetite. Arriving at the restaurant, Ron, Thomas and I exit the car with my security detail.

"Food finally! I'm starving. Who are we having lunch with again?"

"Mr. Marano, Ms. Blackwood," Thomas answers.

I stop walking and take a deep breath; I'm sure he's going to be pissed. While Thomas is squaring things away with the hostess, I look around and my eyes land on a familiar face. Today sucks so fucking bad. It's like everything that could possibly go wrong is going wrong. Faces I never wanted to look at again are being put on full display right in front of me. The hostess walks us over to our party. I look unfazed on the outside, like the bad bitch I am. But on the inside, I feel myself falling apart. I cannot get Samuel off my mind.

"What a pleasant surprise," I say, smiling brightly. "Mr. Marano, Chase. It's been a while." Chase stands, looking at me with indifference. His father on the other hand, stays seated. Ryan pulls my seat out for me, then stands a few feet away on guard, Thomas and Ron take their seats.

"We haven't seen each other in so long and the first thing you do is spout lies. This meeting is neither pleasant, nor is it a surprise. You knew what you were doing when you stole my company."

"Mr. Marano, please. I've had a long day and I'm starving. Let me order first, then we can discuss the crimes you believe I have committed against you," I smile, waving the waiter over. After we order, I look over at Mr. Marano. I know what he's trying to do. He thinks having Chase here will throw me off, he's so wrong. "I did not steal your company, your partner sold it to me legally."

"The only reason he was able to sell it to you was because he tricked me into signing over my shares. I know James, he's not that smart, so that vicious idea had to have come from you."

"Now wait a minute, you're giving me too much credit and underestimating your partner. That was your problem to begin with. You didn't think he had it in him, but you were wrong. Humans betray each other every day." I glance meaningfully at Chase. "I'm sure my secretary has told you that I don't want your company, but it's mine now. I don't plan to break it apart or fire anyone, in fact, you can still run it and keep your title. All I ask is that you keep the company profitable, if it is making money I won't interfere. I'll assign myself the title of chairperson, so from now on you should address me as such."

Mr. Marano's face is beet red; I can tell he wants to attack me. That would be foolish on his part. Ryan is standing behind me with his men deployed around the room. Mr. Marano stands, huffing and puffing as he walks away. That's fine with me, I plan to stay and eat. Luckily, the waitress walks over with our food, I couldn't be happier.

"Did you do it on purpose?" Chase asks. I'd almost forgotten he was still here.

"Did I do what on purpose?" God, I hope he isn't about to hit me with one of his corny pickup lines and ruin my appetite.

"Did you take over my father's company and make him work under you as some sort of revenge against me?" Looking into his eyes, I decide to tell him the truth.

"Even though I didn't want to, I opened myself up to you. I was willing to give you everything. Being betrayed by you almost broke me. This is just the beginning. Until I no longer feel any emotion about it, I plan to take revenge." Chase chuckles.

"You didn't love me, you never loved me. The only one who was betrayed was me. The whole time you were with me, you were thinking about Samuel." I glare at him. "I saw the both of you in the library that day, I almost lost it. But then, I called a friend of mine who went to high school with the both of you and she told me everything. So, don't sit here and think for one minute that I betrayed you, there was nothing to betray, you made sure of that."

"You were fucking those whores before Samuel came along. You don't know me, you don't know what I put myself through to be with you, the fears I faced. You are a fucking coward; I was willing to go against my fucking father for you. I genuinely wanted to love you."

"I introduced you to my fucking parents, we talked about having a future together, having kids." He's shouting now, attracting attention, but I don't care.

"We would have had a future if you weren't such a cheating prick."

"Keep telling yourself that, Ariah. You are a fucking lunatic; you will never be happy. You claim you opened up to me, then you say I don't know you. Which is it, Ariah? How could it be both? I thought you were different, but you're right, I don't know you. The conniving bitch sitting in front of me, is that the real you?" Chase stands, looking down at me as if he's better than me. I'll make him pay for this as well, I think as he storms out. I pick my fork up, thinking about what he just said. The table is awkwardly quiet, but I don't care, nor do I feel embarrassed about what just happened. Maybe I deserve to hear those things from Chase. Fuck Chase. What's done is done.

Once I finish eating, I stand, ready to head back to the office and finish the day. "Ryan, where is he?" I ask, walking out of the restaurant. He opens the car door for me, and I step in.

"He's here. He graduated last month and has been home for two weeks now." Yet another blow I must take to the chest. Is everyone trying to knock me down today? Usually, on a day like this I would call Samuel. I would seek comfort in his words. I can't lose my bullet proof vest, I can't lose Samuel.

Arriving home is not putting my heart at ease like it does every other day. I was able to get through the day without breaking down, but I'm hurt. I know he speaks the truth, my father wouldn't lie to me. We don't lie to each other, which is probably why we don't have deep conversations. He doesn't want to hear my truth and I don't want to hear his. Deciding I don't want to be alone tonight, I head straight to Shelly's room.

Walking in, I hear the shower running so I lay on her bed. I'm sure she's completely insane, but she is still my aunt Shelly. She is the only other person in the world I can talk to who will hug me for as long as I want to be hugged. I hear the shower shut off, moments later the bathroom door opens. I feel a dip in the bed and a gentle hand rubbing my head. The tears I've been holding in all day gushes out of me like a waterfall.

Shelly says nothing as I cry. I am sure she is aware of what's happening. I am afraid to ask her if it's true because I already know the answer. I am afraid of myself, afraid of what I'll do if I see him, afraid of what I'll say when he tells me he's getting married. I'm so stupid, stupid for only one person. I get up and head to my room. Laying down, I stare up at my ceiling and close my eyes.

Waking up, I feel refreshed from all the crying I did last night. I know that I'm not enough for Samuel to go against his father, he showed me that years ago. Honestly, I'm not even sure if I want him to. I don't know if I even have the courage to stand up to Charles Blackwood. The shadows we live under are far too big. If I ever needed to get out, I wouldn't know how. Yawning I sit up, it's time to go to work and deal with whatever is thrown my way.

Chapter Thirteen

"Ms. Blackwood, Mr. Conrad is here," Ron says, peeking his head through the door. I immediately sit up, why would Samuel come to my office? I'm trying to deal with shit on my own, seeing him is just going to fuck up all my hard work.

"Send him in." I remind myself I must keep my emotions in check. The door opens and in walks John.

"My little Ariah, moving up in the world." He looks around my office. "Shit, look at this office! It's fucking huge!" I stand, walking around my desk with a big smile on my face.

"John, it's so nice to see you." I go in for a hug.

"Sure, just like your father, you're hiding how you really feel. I know better, however, I will accept this beautiful smile if you'll have lunch with me."

"What did you have in mind?" My smile is still on my face, I am genuinely happy to see him. If there is anything my godfather is good at, it's keeping a smile on a woman's face.

"Let's go check out my new restaurant. I want you to tell me what you think." I give instructions to Ron. As I am walking out with John, I look towards my father's office. Thomas is sitting at his desk, so I know he's in there. He probably sent John to see how I was doing. The man is childish; however, I will be taking advantage of John's company and the offer of food. I continue walking towards the elevator. I smile, thinking about how happy I am to be getting out of that stuffy office.

A soon as we get outside, John shouts, "Ariah, we're free!" No one on my security detail flinches at his outburst. They've all become accustomed to the crazy, rich, white man who visits the chairman on a regular basis. The car ride is relaxing and comfortable, we talk about random things and people.

The car comes to a stop in front of a grand building. We walk inside and I stop to admire the scene. This place seems over the top, all the waiters, waitresses and hostesses look like models. I feel like I'm on the set of a movie. Gazing around the place I take in all the beautiful artwork displayed. I notice a beautiful woman making her way towards us. I fix my gaze on her as she gets closer, her long blonde hair is pulled to the back of her head and tied in a sleek ponytail. Her cheekbones are high and her legs are long and elegant. Her pale skin looks smooth and soft, not a blemish in sight. For some reason, the closer she gets the more irritated I become. On her dainty left hand, she is wearing a huge ring. A ring that had been placed on my finger before.

I look at John as he watches her. These old bastards are sick. I feel like I'm about to vomit. Why does everything in my life have to be so fucking hard? I'm raging on the inside but looking at me you would never be able to tell. No matter what is thrown in my face, I am still a Blackwood. The beautiful, innocent looking girl finally reaches us.

"Mr. Conrad, we didn't know you were coming. We would've gotten a table ready for you in your private area," she says while hugging him.

"Justine, what have I told you? You're to call me dad, now." Letting her go, John looks at me. "Don't worry about it, me and my goddaughter just wanted to grab lunch and this place came to mind."

"Goddaughter, you have a goddaughter?" she asks as she glances at me.

"Yes, Justine, this is my beautiful goddaughter, the second most beautiful girl in the world, Ariah Blackwood."

"This is Ariah?" She glares at me and I resist the urge to roll my eyes.

"I am." I'm tired of standing here. I put my hand out for her to shake. She takes my hand stiffly.

"So, we're going to be sisters-in-law? I'm Justine Vargo, Samuel's fiancé. I run dad's," she looks at John, "restaurant, for him." Thankfully, she releases my hand. "When it was decided I would marry Samuel, I told them that I didn't just want to be a stay-at-home wife, so Mr- dad, came up with this idea." She talks too fucking much. "Please follow me, I will make sure you guys have a great eating experience." We follow her to a table, Ryan pulls my seat out for me, and I thank him. Little miss sunshine finally walks away. I look at John as he stares at me.

"You and father must be bored these days, what kind of game are the two of you playing?"

"Bored yes, but I'm always bored. What's happening right now is nothing more than the inevitable. Justine and

Samuel have been engaged since before they were born, living the way we live always comes with a price." He picks up his menu, I pick mine up as well. I don't have any more questions, if I open my mouth I'll sound like a fool and embarrass myself. I'm hungry so I should at least eat. There must be something else on John's mind, because he continues looking at me.

"What has your father done to you? If you want to yell and get mad, go ahead, do it. Take all your anger out on me, hate me. Don't sit there and pretend everything is alright, when we both know that's not the case."

Setting my menu down, I give him a long hard stare.

"John, I could never hate you, inevitable, remember? I'm fine, I promise." John sighs and opens his mouth to speak, but before he can get a word out, the waiter walks up. I'm saved for about two seconds.

"Has anyone ever told you how me and your asshole of a father met?" I smile, shaking my head like a little girl.

Going to school day in and day out was like a chore, something I had to do just to make my dying father happy. He had given me a life that others dreamed of, and if you let him tell it, him getting cancer was karma for all the bad shit he'd done in his youth. I was an only child, my parents had me when they were 60 and 25, my father being the elder. According to a maid that helped raise me, my father paid my mother to have me because he needed an heir.

Up until my second year of high school, life was just like everyone else's, boring. I had decided to try something new, spice things up. My friend at the time, Richard, had talked me into trying drugs. Everyone in school was doing them already, I was late to the party. I'd asked him where he was planning to get the drugs from, he then told me of a new scholarship student.

Apparently, while I was daydreaming some new kid had started attending our school and supplied the spoiled, elite minors with all the cocaine they could afford. I was surprised at myself for not being aware of this. I prided myself on knowing everything. But in our circle, there was never anything new to learn. My curiosity got the better of me and I asked Richard to introduce me to this new kid.

"You sure you're up for this? He's not like us and you are kind of an asshole," Richard said, looking me over.

"Richard, what could possibly happen? I have money, he has drugs. This will probably be the dullest meeting I've ever had."

"Here he comes, be chill," Richard said, standing in a relaxed pose. I snickered to myself at Richard's expression.

I must say, I was a bit shocked at our first meeting. His uniform was pristine, he looked clean and a bit nerdy. He was far from the person I had imagined him to be. The person that stood in front of me looked like a dull honor student. I had to stop myself from rolling my eyes. This guy was a drug dealer? Sure, I'd never seen one before, but I'd let my imagination get the best of me and I thought he would be scary.

" Yo, what the fuck ya'll want?" he barked. I raised a brow at the harshness of his tone.

"Is this what drug dealers call good customer service?" Out of the corner of my eye, I saw Richard face palming. Our drug dealer looked over to Richard.

"Hey, white boy, who the fuck is this new white boy you got in my face?" The way he talked and the way he looked had me intrigued.

"My name is John Conrad. I have money and I was under the impression that you have drugs." He looked me dead in the eyes as I spoke. I'd never been intimidated before and I wasn't about to be now.

"You can call me Les," he sized me up. "Have you ever done drugs before, because you don't look like the type." I chuckled.

"Funny you should say that, you don't seem the type to be walking around school with cocaine on you, yet here we are." He didn't say anything to me, he just turned back to Richard.

"Naw white boy, I ain't got nothing for y'all, come see me when you ditch this nigga. Y'all not about to get me fucked over because of an overdose." Then he turned and walked away.

I never did get to try something new that year. Charles refused to sell me drugs, so I stopped asking. I started seeing him around school more often, probably because now I was paying attention. I couldn't understand how this honor student had all the kids afraid of him, had all the teachers love him, while selling drugs. I refused to call him Les, so we never had any conversations. That all changed quickly, like most things.

Richard, who called me his best friend at the time, had been dating Charlotte. Charlotte was the daughter of the school's chairman, so of course, this made her think her shit didn't stink. Like most of the spoiled rich kids, Charlotte developed a drug problem. However, she did not use money to make her purchases, she used her body. I do not think her family was having money problems, I think she just wanted to fuck Charles.

As the only person really paying attention to Charles at the time, I noticed. Charlotte was not discreet about it either. I'm not sure what made me do it, I would usually just watch things from afar as they happened, but not this time. I decided to say something to Les. I sat and waited for him to finish one of his many deals, then ambushed him.

"Yo, Mr. Les," I said in a mocking tone. He was counting his money at the time, when he heard my voice, he reached behind his back. Once he noticed it was me, he went back to counting his money.

"What? I'm not selling yo ass shit."

"Oh, that's not why I'm here. I no longer have the desire to try drugs. Thank you, by the way," he looked up, "for not selling them to me. I feel like you did me a favor, so in

return I wish to pass some information along." He slowly put his money away. "I know about you and Charlotte, and if I know, that means others do too. You should be careful."

"Charlotte?" He seemed puzzled. "Oh, you mean that crackhead that be sucking me off? Man, fuck her! Is that yo girl or something, are you threatening me?" he asked aggressively.

"I don't make threats, like I said, I'm grateful to not be addicted to drugs, this is my repayment. Charlotte does have a boyfriend, Richard, the one you refer to as white boy. Though I'm beginning to believe you don't know any of our names." He shook his head and walked away without responding. I should have left things as they were. Why did I get involved? I don't care about other people. I do not have friends and I hate this school. So why did I even care?

As I predicted, Richard found out about his beloved Charlotte. He reacted like any teenage boy would when they found out the girl they loved was sucking some guy off for drugs. He went bat shit crazy. He confronted her, but of course, she lied. Charlotte promised she would get clean and stay away from drugs. Everyone knew this was a lie as well. This also made Richard want to kill Charles.

"I don't get it, why are you mad at him? Charlotte's not impoverished, so why would she be using her body to get drugs?" We were at my house, Richard had invited himself over to vent.

"I don't know man, all I know is shit didn't start getting fucked up until he brought his poor, black ass to our school." He started pacing the floor. "That scholarship piece of shit thinks he can come to our school and fuck my girl!"

"Maybe your anger is misplaced," I spoke nonchalantly.

"Whose fucking side are you on?" Richard shouted. I looked up from the book I was casually reading.

"No one's. I personally don't care about any of you."

"Then stay out of it unless you're going to help me bring that fucker down."

"Why not get him kicked out of school?"

Richard sat down, "How?"

"How should I know? Let the school find out he's selling drugs or something."

"Shit, that's a great idea. This is why you are my best friend." I rolled my eyes.

"Richard, I'm not your best friend, I barely tolerate you." He ignored my comment.

"I don't even know where he keeps them, how can I tip them off?"

"Tip who off, Richard?"

"The police, I am going to have one of the maids call the cops, tell them that she found drugs in her daughter's room and that her daughter got them from school. Then boom, a locker search."

"Don't you think that's a bit much, I said get him kicked out, not sent to jail."

The next day just like Richard had planned, the police showed up at our school. The teachers had all the students gathered in the gym, while they did their search. I was standing off in a corner by myself just so I could watch everything unfold. Richard was standing with Charlotte, while glaring at Charles. I thought this whole predicament was hilarious. Things would not go the way Richard planned.

After he left my house in a hurry, I couldn't sit and read my book like I had planned. I got in my father's car and found myself in the underdeveloped part of town. I was not sure where I was going or what I was doing. I ended up needing to *stop for gas. I guess my father's Benz stood out, because as soon as I stepped out of the car all eyes were on me. I casually walked into the gas station, bought some gas, then walked back out to my car. As I was pumping gas a group of misfits walked up to me.*

"Yo, white boy, the fuck you doing around here?" This made me laugh, they sounded just like Charles. My laughter must have pissed them off, because one of them pulled a gun on me. I did not jump or act afraid like they expected, I guess it was my foolish arrogance. I did not think I would be dying there, and to be honest, I'm not sure I cared. I finished pumping the gas, then decided to ask them if they knew him.

"Hey, I'm looking for someone named Les. You guys seem like you would know him. Ring any bells?" The guy loosened his grip on the gun and held it at his side.

"You looking for that crazy mothafucka?" I didn't say anything, I just stood there and waited. Some other guy in the group ran over to a payphone and made a call. He walked back over and whispered something in trigger happy guy's ear. "Ok white boy, stay yo ass right here, don't fucking move, if you try to run, imma kill yo ass."

I shrugged my shoulders and leaned back on my father's car. Five minutes later, a car pulled into the gas station and out jumped Mr. Les himself. The driver drove off as he walked over to the scary misfits. I saw them point over to me, and Charles shook his head. They exchanged some weird handshake, then the misfits went on their way. He cautiously walked over to me.

"Now you look like a drug dealer," I stated sarcastically.

"Fuck, you doing around here?" he said, ignoring my comment.

"I'm not sure myself. Richard and I were having this interesting conversation and I thought you would like to know what we were talking about." He stared at me, waiting for me to continue. "Well, our dearest white boy, with my help of course, came up with the idea to get you kicked out. Then somehow, that idea escalated to the police being involved."

"Let me get this straight, you and that nigga trying to get me kicked out? Then, you flip on your boy and come tell me. How I know you ain't lying? I should let my young boys come over here, beat yo ass then take this fucking ride."

"Well Mr. Les, I don't lie. People lie because they fear others knowing the truth, I fear nothing. Send your 'young boys' as you put it over here, I'm sure me and my ride will make it home safely."

He glared at me while I glared at him. I didn't like being threatened, which is why I myself did not use threats. I am a man of action. Sure, I was being underestimated because of how I looked, but none of that mattered. I would surely kill anyone who threatened my life. Charles looked at me with understanding, because for the first time he smiled at me.

"I knew you were crazy. Alright John, you got it; I believe you." With that, he walked off.

Now here we all were in the gym waiting for this police search to be over. I wondered what he would do with the information I had given him. Was he as smart as I thought he was, or had I wasted my time? Thirty minutes went by, before finally, the chairman walked in with the police behind him. He walked right over to Charlotte and smacked her. The police took her into custody, then they also arrested Richard. The look on their faces were priceless. The police had found large amounts of drugs in both of their lockers. I looked over to Charles and he gave me a slight nod. I did enjoy the show he put on.

Two weeks later, both Richard and Charlotte were back at school. It was like it never happened, but we knew it did and the tension in the air around school was thick. One day, while sitting in one of the classrooms, I was reading a magazine while Richard and Blake, another nobody, carried on a conversation.

"I just don't get it Richard, how did the drugs get into your locker?" asked Blake.

"The fuck should I know, my parents are mad as fuck. My dad took away my fucking keys and Charlotte's dad is forbidding her from seeing me. Everything is fucked."

"Well, who knew about your plans?" Blake asked. I was getting annoyed; they had been having this same conversation for an hour.

"I told Charles about your dumb plan Richard, get over it." They both looked over at me.

"What do you mean, John? Why the fuck would you do that?" Richard was now in my face. "I know you're crazy, but how could you do that to me?" I shrugged.

"I thought it would be amusing and it was." I went back to my magazine. Richard grabbed me by the collar, while Blake grabbed him by his shoulders.

"He's not worth it dude, let's go. You know how deranged he is." Richard let me go, then they both walked out. The room was quiet, just the way I liked it. I heard a tap on the door, I looked up and there stood Charles.

"My goodness John, you are something else. How could you treat your friends like that?" He walked into the classroom, disturbing my peace.

"I don't have friends, they are just people that help the day go by." I was becoming annoyed once again.

"You know, I've been trying to figure you out. I know why they fear me, but why do they fear you?" I smirked and turned a page in my magazine.

"Haven't you heard? I'm crazy, deranged. Anyway, you shouldn't be worried about me. Richard is going to retaliate, so good luck." He started to walk out the door.

"If anyone should watch out, it should be him cause I'm not done with him."

The next few weeks proved to be very entertaining. Charles would provoke Richard, Richard would react, usually by making a fool of himself. Why didn't he just let it go? To make matters worse, Charlotte had begun openly dating Charles. It was hilarious that even the chairman approved of their relationship. Maybe that was why Richard could not let it go.

I guess Richard had enough of being a laughingstock because he challenged Charles to fight one on one. Charles decided to oblige. Why? I will never know. Charles was merciless and proceeded to beat the shit out of Richard. I stood against the wall watching, I was thoroughly entertained like everyone else. The coward within him emerged, and Richard pulled out a pocketknife.

"Richard's got a knife," I sang out loud and clear.

A tussle began and Richard ended up with the knife stuck in his leg. Teachers finally showed up when it was all said and done. The police were called, and Charles was placed in handcuffs. Richard spun the story as if he were the victim to the crazed, poor, black scholarship student who attacked him out of jealousy. I couldn't listen to the nonsense any longer.

"Hey, Richard was the one with the knife. He also attacked the scholarship student." That was all it took, I

guess the other students were tired of Richard, because they all started speaking up. Charles was then released and told to go home for the day. Richard looked at me with blazing fire in his eyes. I shrugged my shoulders like I always did and walked away. As I was leaving to head back into school, I felt someone's arm go around my shoulder.

"You one crazy ass white boy John and I like it." I pushed his arm off my shoulder.

"Look, I don't do friends." He smiled at me.

"Me either, John. I have decided that you will be my brother from another mother. Come on, give me a ride home so you can meet the rest of the family."

Chapter Fourteen

"And just like that, I was a part of the family. Charles said I saved his life, I once asked him what he meant. He explained to me that if he had gotten kicked out of school, he would have been in the streets. But because of me, he was able to graduate from that private school, go to a good college and make something of himself. He gives me too much credit. I was just bored. I did not know what a family was, I barely saw my father and I was always alone. So, I have always been thankful to Charles and Michelle for accepting all of me. It's a great story, right?" John asks cheerfully. I take a bite of the food in front of me, it's already almost cold because I was so engrossed in the story.

"John, you were a weird teenager."

"I was." Before I can say anything else, Justine walks over and takes a seat.

"How is everything? You guys look like you were having a great conversation, what was it about?"

"I was just telling Ariah the story of how I met her father." I continue eating as they engage in small talk. I need to focus on my food so I don't have to look at Justine with that ring on her finger. Why did he give her that ring? Couldn't he have bought her a new one? Thinking about it makes me want to just kill Samuel. I can clearly remember the day he placed that ring on my finger.

We had just had sex. As usual, John and my father had gone on a business trip. We left school mid-way because we could not keep our hands off each other. While laying on the bed, Samuel reached over and took something from his pants pocket.

"Ariah, give me your hand," he held his hand out. I gave him my hand and he placed a diamond ring on my finger. I had never seen anything like it before. We had agreed not to fully commit to each other for obvious reasons, so I did not understand what was happening. I just stared at my hand, admiring the ring. I did not know what to say.

"I'm not giving it to you, not yet anyway. This ring belonged to my mother. It is the only thing I have left of her. The woman I marry is going to wear this ring. I wanted to see what it would look like on your finger. I have to put it back

though, before my father finds out I took it and kill me." He
took my hand and kissed it. "It's perfect."

I feel myself getting worked up, interrupting their
conversation, I politely excuse myself from the table. I
quickly find the sign for the restroom. I go into a stall and
lock the door. Why am I having an attack right now? I clutch
my chest trying to control my breathing, but everything
feels like it's spinning. Placing my hand on the wall for
balance I close my eyes. *"Just breathe Ariah, deep breaths,"* I
tell myself. *"You cannot cry, you have made it this far, calm
down."*

Once I have everything under control, I exit the stall
to wash my hands. I look at myself in the mirror. As usual,
my reflection is perfect. I must never be seen as anything
else but perfect. I have the world at my fingertips, I just
have to reach out and grab it. The restroom door opens and
little miss sunshine herself walks in.

"Oh, Ariah I was just coming to check on you." I smile.
I am not sure if I want to be cordial to her or if I want to let
her know I don't like her. Justine walks over, looking in the
mirror at herself. She stretches her hand out and admires
her ring. "Ariah, you and Samuel are close, right?" I stare at

her reflection in the mirror blankly. "I'm just saying this for your own good, maybe you shouldn't stick so closely to a man who's about to get married. People may start spreading gossip." Blowing herself a kiss, she skips out the door. I am speechless. It's been a long time since someone surprised me. Did I just get checked? Did Justine just put me in my place? I dry my hands then return to the table to finish my lunch. While John debates if he wants dessert or not, I have a thought.

"John, why did you bring me here?" I didn't care at first, but after leaving the restroom I'm curious. John looks up from the menu smiling.

"I thought you would never ask. Any woman who is going to be in Samuel's life has to be aware of your existence."

"I was brought here to test little miss sunshine?" What am I to these people?

"You could say that. I knew how you would react, but how would she? I told her you are the love of his life. I also told her that you also once wore that ring." These old bastards.

"Is there anything about me and Samuel that you and my father don't know?"

"No," he goes back to looking at the menu.

"Maybe I'll take you up on your offer." I feel my eyes start to water.

"Which one?"

"The one where I hate you." John chuckles.

"You can't break right now. Keep it up, you've been doing great." I blink back the tears, then I smile at him. "That's my girl. I've decided, let's have dessert." Little miss sunshine walks back to our table.

"Have you guys decided on dessert?" I take the menu from John's hand.

"We have, we will have the chocolate cake." I hand the menus to her. John smiles at me, he reaches across the table and grabs my hand. Little miss sunshine sees this, then walks away. I cannot tell if he is doing this to comfort me or to get on her nerves, either way I need it. I also must think of a way to get that bitch back for the words that flew from her mouth in the restroom. I am sad and emotionally fucked at the moment, but who the fuck does she think she is fucking with?

I have had enough for the day. After lunch with John, I just want to be alone. I text Ron and tell him to reschedule my appointments, then I turn my phone off. If I do not show up to the office, my father will be pissed, but I do not care. I do not want to go home; I'll just get some fresh air. The sun is shining, it has been a while since I sat outside. Taking a seat on a vacant park bench, I take a deep breath then exhale.

I find myself thinking of my mother. Whenever bad thoughts get the best of me, I think of her. If I ever see her again, I will probably try to kill her. My emotional damage began with her. Why is it that no matter what happens in my life I feel like a victim? I can cry everyday about what happened to me when I was a child, I can cry about losing my child, I can cry about being betrayed repeatedly. But what will my tears change?

I am still tainted, I am still childless, I will still be alone. I can throw myself pity parties, I can tell people my story and have them join in. But then who would I be? I do not have a choice but to hold my shit together. No matter how much my tears want to escape, I must hold them in. Even when everything around me is falling apart, I must still keep it together. I can no longer depend on Samuel. I need to depend on myself.

I feel a tear slide down my cheek. I wipe it away. I must wipe my own tears now. I cannot allow myself to forgive him. I feel like a fool once again. Chase is right, I will never be happy. Samuel being my weakness ends right now. Even though I am afraid to let go of the light he became for me, I am Ariah Blackwood. I can't be a mistress; I will not take second place to anyone. Another tear makes its way down my face.

I hate Samuel Conrad. He should have left me alone. I didn't need him to come back into my life, only to leave and hurt me this much. Why did he have to be my savior? Why did I fall for him so hard? Everything that I have given him I'm taking back. He can no longer have all of me. Right here, on this park bench will be the last time I cry for him. Samuel does not deserve me. I feel a presence next to me, I look over and see a handsome Asian man staring at me.

"Sorry if I scared you, you looked like you were deep in thought," his voice is deep and clear. As I breathe air into my lungs, the scent of his cologne tickles my nostrils. I smile at the stranger.

"I was giving myself a pep talk, I am my own cheerleader." He laughs loudly.

"Well, you look extremely happy, so I guess it worked, or are you a good liar?" I look at him, intrigued.

"Maybe? I guess you will have to find out." Am I flirting? I stand quickly. "So, I'll be on my way." I attempt to walk past him, but he grabs my hand. I look down at his hand touching mine, then I look at him.

"I wanted to add to your cheer, GOOD LUCK!" he says, letting my hand go. As I walk away, I hear him yell, "see you later love." I do not look back, I continue on my way. I feel refreshed, I think I am ready to let Samuel go. I know it will take more time, but it must be done.

Walking up to the car, I smile at Ryan. "Change of plans, let's go back to the office." I get in as he closes the door.

Walking out of the elevator, I see Ron packing up his things ready to leave.

"Ms. Blackwood, I thought you were done for the day?" I smile at him.

"You can go. I just need to look over a few things."

"If you are here, then I am here." I giggle.

"Go home Ron, that is an order." Ron slowly makes his way onto the elevator, staring at me. Once the doors close, I walk into my office and take off my suit jacket. I kick my heels off, slide into my pink plush slippers then take a seat in my big comfortable chair. First things first, I need to drown myself in work, this way I won't have time to think about Samuel. I should think of someone else in his place, maybe I'll think of that handsome Asian guy that cheered me on at the park.

He can be my imaginary perfect boyfriend, the one I fell in love with in high school. The one my father approves of, the one who never betrayed me. I sound insane, but I must do what I must to not be damaged by all this. I need to give him a name. I lean back in my chair. Since he is not real, I can call him anything, I will call him Dumpling. It's a bit racist, but I like it.

I turn my laptop on and get to work. I let myself fall behind, but not anymore. I cannot let anything or anyone get in my way anymore. I am a big girl. I will get over this heartbreak, I have gotten over much worse. To the world, I am an intelligent, beautiful, successful heir with the world at my fingertips. But all I want is to love and be loved in return. I am not over the things that have traumatized me, but I must move on.

I will never give anyone the kind of power I gave to Samuel. I will lock all the bad shit away, all the memories, everything. This is just another thing in my life that I will survive. Besides, I have Dumpling now. I laugh to myself; I must be bat shit crazy. It's his fault, he should have never wished me good luck, now he's stuck in my head. I arrive home in time for dinner. I'm pleased that I was able to get a lot of work done. I send Ron a text with instructions on what needs to be done for the week. I feel like the boss that I am. When I walk into the dining room, Shelly and my father are flirting with each other. I clear my throat to let them know I am in the room.

"Ariah, we've been waiting," Shelly says, her face glows with happiness. I don't say anything, I just take a seat. I'm jealous of her, not for the usual, but because she looks genuinely happy to be with the person she loves. Right now, I hate everyone.

"I hear you've met Justine," the old bastard speaks.

"Justine?" My aunt looks between my father and me. "Who's Justine?"

"Samuel's fiancé," I answer, staring at the table.

"Where on earth would you have had the chance to run into her?" This time my father beats me to it.

"John and Ariah had lunch today. He took her to his new restaurant; Justine manages it for him."

"Since when do you talk so much? Why do I get the feeling you and John are acting like children? Why would he take Ariah there?" She takes the words right out of my mouth.

"She would need to meet her one way or another. Ariah needs reality to be placed in front of her. I want her to understand, she doesn't need any false hope." The maids bring our dinner in. The tension in the room is stifling. My aunt is glaring daggers at my father, I on the other hand, am over it. I gave myself all day to get over it. Before Shelly can begin her rage filled rant, I cut her off.

"Yes, it was something that would happen eventually. I am fine Shelly, I promise. She is a nice girl, of course I don't like her. She's not stealing Samuel away from me, he's walking away on his own."

"But Ariah-," before my aunt can finish, my father cuts her off.

"He was not someone you could claim in the first place." I look at him with raised brows. "Think about it, has he contacted you? Why? Because John told him not to. The moment John told him he could not have you, he accepted it. I don't understand why you are being so stubborn." I casually pick up my wine glass.

"I feel like you're challenging me, Father. How should I take it?" I ask sipping some wine.

"Ariah."

"I said I was fine, but now you're telling me that I have no claim over him, when we all know that's a lie. If there is anything in this world that I can have, whenever I want, however I want, it is Samuel. We play by the rules you and John have laid down, but that is by choice."

I stop myself before things get too heated. I have never disrespected my father and I do not want to start now. I feel like the only way I will get over my father and little miss sunshine's words is to fuck Samuel on his wedding day. I could call Samuel now, but I am not going to do that. Not because of my father or John, but because of me. Samuel has never fought for me, and now I no longer want him to.

Time waits for no one; it flies by and without notice you can lose it. My work is nonstop, I am grateful for this. It is the only thing I focus on. I think of my Dumpling telling me good luck every now and then, he is so sweet. I have not seen or spoken to Samuel and I do not plan to. Today is a normal day for me, I have had meetings after meetings, and now I am having take-out. As I scroll through my schedule for the week, trying to figure out what I can ditch or put on the back burner, I hear a light knock on the door. Ron peeks in.

"Ms. Blackwood, I know you're eating lunch, but there's a Ms. Vargo here to see you. When I tried to have her leave, Thomas told me to let you know she was here first." Today is not the day for this bullshit. "Let her in."

Moments later the door opens and there she stands. I refuse to be nice to her because I do not like her. She can stand there for all I care; she even has the nerve to disturb my lunch.

"No smile? Sheesh, I thought we could at least be nice to one another." She walks over and takes a seat on my couch. I smile to myself; this bitch is crazy. "I came because I have two questions I must ask." I say nothing as I stare at her. "Have you spoken to Samuel lately?" I don't know what she's playing at, but I guess I'll play along.

"No Justine, I have not spoken to Samuel, not in months actually." She awkwardly looks around my office.

"Joh- or dad rather, has asked me, to ask you if you would like to be a bridesmaid in the wedding. If you could just say no to this question as well, I will be on my way."

Replaying what she just said in my head gives me an idea. I give her a sweet smile as I respond, "sure Justine, I'll be a bridesmaid."

Justine's eyes widen in alarm. "Why would you want to be in my wedding?"

"Why not?" I hold her gaze in a challenging manner.

She stands to leave, "I'll have someone contact Ron with the details." Once she is out the door, I start feeling dizzy. Everything around me seems to be moving in a circular motion. I feel like throwing my lunch up. Clenching my fists, I can feel my nails sinking into my skin. This helps me to calm down. Why did I agree? Why do I always have to take the hard path? Opening my hands, I take deep breaths, what did I just get myself into?

Chapter Fifteen

Could my life be more depressing? Lying in bed, I look over at my phone that has not stopped vibrating for the past month due to little miss sunshine and her mother's never-ending texts. Hilariously enough, I have been bumped up from bridesmaid to maid of honor. This is probably John's doing, I don't care to ask why, it will just piss me off. One day I will pay these old bastards back for the games they continuously play.

The main question I have been asking myself is, why the hell is Justine going along with this shit? She is aware of me and Samuel's relationship, why the fuck would she want me in her wedding? This shit is not making sense. Then again, when does anything in my life ever make sense? Agreeing to be in the wedding seems to have put my father at ease. He doesn't bother me about Samuel anymore, but Shelly is worried.

I have told her countless times that I am all right and that I do not need to talk about it, but she isn't satisfied with that. Every time I come home from an event I have had to attend with Justine, she is waiting at the door asking me if I talked to him. My answer is always the same, no. Justine is a smart woman; she knows I'm being forced on her and she is doing a fantastic job of making sure Samuel and I are never in the same room.

It has been about eight months since I have seen or even spoken to him, I'm grateful for that. This past month has helped me prove to myself that I can do anything. There have been times when we were in the same place, but I didn't avoid or react, I just let things flow the way Justine wanted them to. She and her annoying mother are easy people to ignore. Claire Vargo is a woman who prides herself on being kept. When I first met her, I thought I'd have to kill her. She went on and on about how I was far too beautiful to be working so hard for my father and that I should kick back, enjoy life and let a man take care of me.

In my mind, I thought that's what I had been doing all these years. I thought I was leaning on Samuel and my father too much for that matter. Apparently, in her eyes, I am too independent. Claire texts me daily with updates on the different things they have picked for the wedding. I told them both that I would not be able to attend every tasting or viewing, but if they sent me texts with pictures, I would give my opinion.

Today unfortunately, is not a text day. Today is the last fitting for the dresses and I must be in attendance. Up until today, I had been doing everything I should as a maid of honor. Luckily, they decided to not have a bachelorette party. I'm sure I would have attempted suicide or murder if I had to pretend to like her for too long. Getting out of bed, I walk into the bathroom and turn on the shower. Today is going to be a long day.

Walking into the kitchen in my robe, I grab a muffin off the counter. Jumping on the counter, I relax. Surprisingly, the kitchen is empty and quiet. I am starting to hate when it's quiet. Enjoying the moistness of my muffin, my father and Shelly walk in laughing. I roll my eyes; I hate happy people as well.

"Good morning Ariah, I thought you'd be on your way to work by now," Shelly says pinching my thigh as she walks by.

"Not today, I have to go get fitted for my dress. The wedding is next week."

Shelly looks between my father and me. "Are you really going through with this?"

"She is, she said yes so she must follow through with it," my father says looking down at his phone.

"Charles-"

I cut her off, "he's right. Plus, I want a front row seat to this betrayal." I hop off the counter, leaving before either of them can respond. I know what I said, I know what I keep telling myself, but part of me is hoping Samuel will call the wedding off. Walking into my closet to get dressed, I stop to look at myself in the mirror. *"You got this,"* I say to myself. Ariah Blackwood can survive anything.

"Oh Ariah, we may have to change your dress. We can't have you upstaging Justine," Claire says as she takes another sip of wine.

I don't say anything, I just smile, looking at myself in the mirror. I am not surprised I look perfect; I always look perfect. The curtains next to me open and out steps Justine. Her puffy dress makes her look like one of the princesses in the fairytales my mother use to read to me. She genuinely looks happy. I feel myself becoming sad, but I must keep this ungodly smile on my face.

Justine looks over to me, "Ariah, what do you think? Will Samuel like it? I can't wait for him to take it off on our honeymoon." I stare at her as she turns back to her mother. "Mother, what do you mean change dresses? Ariah will look beautiful in anything, even my wedding dress," she looks at me, smirking.

I smooth my dress out, while looking at myself. I must make sure my feelings are not showing on my face and sure enough, I look pleasant and unaffected. How could I let my guard down? I almost forgot who this bitch truly was. I must see this bull shit to the end.

"Justine, you look like a princess out of a fairytale. I know Samuel, I know him really well," I make sure to pause on that part, "he won't be able to take his eyes off you," I say truthfully.

"No, he won't, you look gorgeous darling," Claire chimes in.

Justine openly glares at me for the first time, but I ignore her and continue smiling. Before the store clerk can close my curtain so I can get out of the dress, John walks in.

Everything starts to move in slow motion, why right now? Samuel walks in behind his father. He's changed so much since the last time I saw him. He let his facial hair grow out, his hair is a mess, a good mess though, one he would have never walked around with before. He doesn't see me, which is weird for me because no matter what, whenever he walked into a room I was in, his eyes would automatically find mine. Samuel looks at Justine and smiles, she is the only person he sees.

I'm as still as a statue. I knew things would be like this, which is why I did not want to see him. I stare at him like a deer in the headlights. Our eyes meet and unlike any other time I cannot stop my eyes from watering. I watch as Justine and Claire walk over to him, I watch as they talk to him fondly. I watch as they stand next to each other, looking happy. During this whole exchange, Samuel sneaks glances my way. The smile he walked in with is gone. A tear slips down my face, and out of nowhere the curtain is closed abruptly.

I can hear John telling Justine how beautiful she looks and I am grateful for the distraction. I am sure that at any moment, Justine and Claire would have wanted to know what had Samuel's attention and would have looked in my direction. They would have turned to see me standing there crying pathetically. The clerk helps me out of the dress and into my clothes. I look at myself in the mirror, wipe my tears, gather my confidence then walk out. Claire, Justine and Samuel are no longer in the room, John stands alone waiting for me.

"I'm sorry, honey bunches, I didn't know you would be here. Usually, Justine would have had you gone before we showed up."

I shake my head, "I'm fine I promise. I'm glad I got that over with."

John walks up with open arms, I hug him as tight as I can. He pulls away looking down at me.

"The most beautiful girl in the world," he says, pushing my hair behind my ear.

"What about Shelly?" I ask, laughing.

"She got old."

Today is the big day, I lay lazily in bed looking at the ceiling. I should run away. Why did I choose to be there? I look over to my nightstand at my phone, should I call Samuel? Should I give in and just beg him not to do this? Seeing him last week made me think of all the memories we share; he is all I know. I place my pillow over my head and scream into it. I will call him, and we can just leave all this shit behind. What about our happy ending? Those old fucks live their lives the way they want, why can't we? There is a knock on the door, before I can say come in, it opens and in walks my father. I pull my knees to my chest, I cannot look at him. Silently, he takes a seat on the edge of my bed.

"You never said if you liked your room." I do not say anything. He has not been home for the past couple of days, and the first thing he does when he comes back is come to my room to talk nonsense.

"Daddy, I love everything you give me; you only give me the best," I say sarcastically. He stands and looks down at me.

"Don't hate me for too long. Everything I do, I do to make sure you'll be able to survive long after I'm gone." He looks away from me. Walking over to my couch, he picks up an old teddy bear. "Do you know where this came from?"

"No," I stand up, walking over to him.

"The first week you were here, you wouldn't sleep. I called John, thinking he would know what to do since he had a kid," he chuckles. "That bastard yelled at me telling me he clearly didn't know shit about girls which is why his wife killed herself." He shakes his head at the memory. "He told me to buy you a teddy bear 'girls like that shit right'? That night, I had one of the maids bring it to you. I could tell you still didn't trust me. They reported to me the next day that you slept through that whole night like a baby." Handing me the teddy bear, I place it back on the couch. "I'm sorry for telling you 'no'." He looks into my eyes. "John told me about what happened last week." He lifts his hand to my face, brushing my cheek lightly. "No more tears, Ariah. Do not waste another tear." Why is he doing this to me? "You are worth more than that," he says sternly before leaving.

Like the hero he is, he came and saved me. I was going to call Samuel and beg him to run away with me, but why should I have to beg? Fuck that, I am worth fighting for.

If Samuel cannot see that, then fuck him. I still have some time left before the wedding. I don't want to be there early, I just want to stand there and get it over with. Falling into my bed, I close my eyes. Maybe this is all just some horrible dream. My phone begins ringing, letting me know that this is my reality.

"Hello," I answer, annoyed.

"Oh Ariah, I'm glad you picked up. This is Claire, darling. I know you said you would be here a little later, but we need you. Everything is a mess. The flowers are wrong and Justine is freaking out. Also, it would seem the French chef you hired will only listen to you. Please darling, come down at once."

I look at my phone pissed. "Sure thing Claire, I'll be there shortly." If I could wring my own neck, I would. I basically planned this damn thing. Justine and her mother wouldn't know class if it knocked them over the fucking head. Like my father said, I already agreed and if I am going to do something, I am going to do it fucking right. Even if it's killing me on the inside. I reluctantly walk into the bathroom and turn the shower on. Staring at myself in the mirror, I feel like clawing my own eyes out. I feel so fucking frustrated with myself, with Samuel, my father, John and even Shelly. Stepping into the shower, I wish the water would wash all my pain away.

What is my life? I feel like Samuel is my life, even when I left and we were apart for two years, he was still a part of me. Walking into my closet, I put on some sweats. My life is a fucking joke, everyone must be laughing at me. Who in their right mind would agree to be a part of this circus? Walking to my car, Ryan opens the door for me, and I get in. While driving, Ryan continuously glances back at me through the rearview mirror.

"Ryan, do you have something you want to say?" I ask, looking down at my hands. They can't seem to stop moving.

"Ariah, I've been with you a long time," he pauses. "If anyone outside the two of you know what your relationship is, I think that would be me."

"That's right. You're the one person who knows everything."

"So, excuse me, I'm sure it's not my place." I look up. "Why haven't you asked him not to go through with this? I know you; you wouldn't ask something like that over the phone. I also know you haven't gone to see him."

I look out the window, staring at nothing at all. I think seriously about his question. So many times, I've been tempted to call him, wanting to see him. I find myself missing him, wanting to know why he is doing this to me. Samuel knows that I will be hurt by this. He knows that he is everything to me, so why? Ryan has been around to witness everything, I am sure he had to write thorough reports for my father.

"I'm not enough," I say out loud. I am not enough, I was not back then, and I am not now. Stopping at a red light, Ryan meets my eyes in the mirror and I can tell he knows exactly what I mean. There is no need for any more words to be said.

Arriving at the hotel, I take a deep breath. I must make sure Samuel has a perfect wedding with someone else. As I step out the car, Claire rushes to meet me, her face is flushed and filled with worry.

"Thank goodness! I don't know what to do. She won't stop crying." We begin walking through the hotel. "Look at the flowers, what is that? Her hair is not looking the way she wants it, and that damned chef!"

I grab her shoulders, "Claire, calm down." She takes a deep breath. "Go calm your daughter down, I will call someone for her hair. Don't worry about anything else, I'll take care of it. After all, I am the maid of honor." I walk her towards the elevators. "People will start to show up in about an hour, you need to change into your gown." I pull my phone out and send a quick text. "Robin will be here in about 15 minutes to work on Justine's hair. She does my hair, so she's highly recommended. This will be a perfect day for your daughter." The elevator doors open, I push her into it. "Get up there and assure Justine that everything is going to be perfect."

Claire smiles at me, I smile back. The doors close and I drop the act. I will be glad when this shit is fucking over. I walk into the kitchen first, apparently dumb and dumber were trying to change the menu today. I tell the chef not to worry and to do everything as planned. I also call Tom to have him bring new ingredients and make the menu additions that they want to add.

As for the flower situation, there is nothing I can do. These are the flowers that we agreed on, I guess with Claire's old age she is forgetting things. I will have the florist set them up accordingly. Things are not as bad as she made them seem. I took care of the "problems" in minutes. I head to my hotel room to hide away from everyone. Robin stops by to let me know the bride's hair is done. She then asks about my hair. I tell her I will pull it back into a bun, nothing fancy.

Standing in my bra and underwear, I look in the mirror. What is so wrong with me? Why doesn't anyone ever choose me? Will I ever be someone's number one? Will I one day be someone's everything? I hear my room door unlock, why would someone else have my room key? Who is interrupting my pity party? I turn, staring at the door, not thinking to cover my body. He walks in, closing the door quickly. Pressing his back against the door, he stares directly into my soul.

Why is he here? What the fuck is happening? Samuel is standing before me in his tux. He looks ready to tell another woman "I do". I can't find any words, I can't move, I seem to have forgotten how to breathe. Even after everything this asshole has put me through, I am still weak for him. He takes a step towards me, I put my hands up, shaking my head no. If he gets close to me, I am one hundred percent sure I will give in.

Ignoring my pleas, he proceeds. The closer he gets, the more tears fall. Samuel is trying to kill me, that must be it. That must be the reason he will not allow me to get over him in peace. Standing in front of me, he looks down into my eyes as I look up into his. I want to ask him why, but before I can say anything, he puts his hand over my mouth. I close my eyes, take a deep breath and inhale his smell, something I haven't been able to do in a long time. Opening my eyes, I see tears coming down his face as well.

Pushing his hand away, I quickly attack his lips. Jumping into his arms, I kiss him as if my life depends on it. The tears will not stop as he holds me tightly, my legs are wrapped around him, holding on for dear life. All the pain I've been feeling, all the insecurities, everything, I am putting them all on him. I don't care if he is hurt about the situation, I don't want to see things from his point of view.

Right now, I want to feel better, I want to escape. Kissing Samuel with all my heart makes my mind turn to mush. Our bodies are at war with one another as we try to get closer. I kiss and bite his neck, then his chest. I want to leave my mark. I want to show the world that at one point in time, he was mine.

Sitting down on the bed with me still in his arms, his movements become rough, there will be hickies all over. Flipping me on my back, he pulls my panties down. Then he immediately puts his face between my legs. He takes me to that euphoric place that only he has directions to. I grab the sheets tightly. All the memories of us having sex comes flooding in. All the good times we've had together, all the pain we've caused each other, everything about us.

Reaching my orgasm, "Samuel," I scream with tears streaming down my face.

Making his way up my body, he leaves a trail of kisses. Usually I let him have control, but not this time. Flipping our bodies so that I am on top, I ease my way down onto his shaft. Sitting still, I look Samuel dead in his eyes. I fell in love with these beautiful blue eyes. Slowly, I rotate my hips in a circular motion, the same way he taught me all those years ago. Everything I know about pleasure, I learned from him. Speeding up, he manages to hit all my favorite spots. He tightens his grip on my waist. Putting my hands on his chest, I make sure to keep my eyes from his. I am losing my mind. Tears fall on his chest; the emotional pain is too much. Samuel is looking up at me with eyes that show pity. I hit his chest hard.

"How could you do this to me? Why are you abandoning me?" Speeding up, I wrap my hands around his neck. "Tell me you love me. Tell me no matter what, I'm the only person in the world you'll ever love." He is quietly taking everything I am laying on him. "Tell me you love me." I feel like a crazy woman, I feel psychotic. Sitting up he hugs me close; I don't stop moving my hips.

"Three words, eight letters," I whisper. Samuel flips me onto my back, I hold him close, so I don't have to see his face.

"What good would those words do?" This is the first time I have heard Samuel's voice in almost a year. Pumping into me slowly, he takes control. I want to fight it, but my body won't listen. He moves in for a kiss, I turn my head, so he kisses my neck instead. I close my eyes tightly as I feel it, that pure, hateful ecstasy. My whole body begins to shake. I bite into his shoulder as my nails dig into his back. Why does it have to feel so good? I ride this feeling out slowly, savoring the last time.

I open my eyes to Samuel looking down at me, kissing my forehead he gets out the bed. I am the only one who climaxed. Was this only charity sex? I laugh hysterically at myself. Samuel slides his tux back on. Grabbing my phone, I make sure Robin is still around, I need her after all. Tossing my phone, I head to the shower. Before I make it into the bathroom, he grabs my arm. I try to pull away and fail. He pulls me close, my back to his chest, then wraps his arms around my waist and breast.

"Forget me Ariah, I'm a coward. I'm not someone who has what it takes to love you forever," he whispers as he lightly kisses my shoulder. I lean my head back into him, staring at the bathroom door. Turning around, I put my face into his chest and take a deep breath. He smells like me, I no longer smell his scent, there is only mine. I look up at him with tear filled eyes.

"Tell me you love me." I desperately want to hear it.

"You are the only woman I will ever love. I love you, Ariah Blackwood." His hand caresses my face, I lean into it.

"Good," I begin choking up. "Suffer forever. Remember that you can never have me while still loving only me." I push away from him, walking into the bathroom to shower.

The wedding occurred without a hitch, I planned everything perfectly. One would think Samuel and I are strangers. We didn't talk or even look at each other throughout the whole ceremony. When Justine turned for me to hold her bouquet, I took it with a smile. I fixed her train; I handed her a handkerchief for her fake tears. I was the perfect maid of honor. After all, I excel at anything I do.

Now here we are, at the reception. Justine and Claire were satisfied with the menu. The Bride and Groom had their first dance, the photographer took many pictures as they happily cut the cake. My job is now done. It is time for me to go. I am finally done with this whole debacle. I walk around the hall looking for my father. I find him talking to a business colleague. I don't feel like talking, so I take a seat at a random table waiting for him to finish. Little miss sunshine takes a seat beside me.

"My mother told me you fixed everything, I just wanted to say thank you before you left." I stay quiet, she looks down at her ring. "I won," she looks up at me. "Everyone told me that you would be this hard opponent. They said that I should watch out and that you were not easy. Looks like they were wrong, you are just a daddy's girl, after all. You gave Samuel up without a fight and now I have the ring." I am sick of this bitch.

"So how do I taste?"

"Excuse me?" she asks, confused.

"When you stood in front of everyone you know, everyone you love, and kissed your husband, how did I taste? No matter how hard you try to pretend you didn't notice, I know you saw those hickies on his neck." I scoot closer to her. "Right before your wedding, I fucked your husband, his face was between my legs and he was eating like a starved child. Then do you know what he did after that? He came downstairs and married you. He kissed you with my pussy still on his lips." Her face turns beet red, but

I'm not done. "Listen up sunshine, Samuel is a man that I can have access to whenever I want. Remember this fact the next time you challenge me."

Looking at her shocked face is satisfying. I am done. I will put all this bull behind me. I stand, leaving her with her thoughts. Outside, Ryan is holding the car door open for me. I have a lot of work to catch up on, so I tell him to take me to the office. My life will go on, life always goes on. I will protect myself from now on, all I need is me. Oh, and Dumpling of course, I smile. I'm sorry I cheated on you Dumpling; it will never happen again.

Chapter Sixteen

One year later...

"Ron, why the fuck have I not been updated on London yet?" I stare at him. If I have to put up with these imbeciles in this board room for a second longer, I may take Ryan's gun and shoot them.

"If we had moved quicker, they wouldn't have been able to get in contact with them. I knew this would happen." Matt from wherever the fuck has a lot of fucking nerve.

"Mam-," I cut Ron off.

"Don't repeat that bull shit, Ron. Tell the fucker who spoke out of turn, I wasn't talking to him. I know all the bastards who work for me and I only have one person in this room named Ron. Also, who the fuck is he talking to? Did I not make myself clear earlier?" These idiots are trying to run my company like children, so I plan to treat them as such. They had one fucking job while I went to Mexico for a development project. I asked them to make sure a shitty company I wanted to buy did not get any new contracts. All they had to do was be a brick wall, I had so many plans for Brooke Co., but with this new contract they may be getting in London, they will no longer need to sell. Fuck! I take a deep breath. "Ron, who is Brad's main contact in London?"

Ron looks over at Matt from wherever the fuck, "Matt, do we know who they're signing the contract with?"

"No, not yet. I have my people looking into it as we speak. My contact believes it was someone from their government." Ron looks at me, before he can repeat the answer, I put my hand up. I close my eyes, thinking of a plan. I cannot rely on these fuckers. My thoughts are interrupted as they always are in these meetings.

"Why do we have to keep going after them? We've used enough resources on them, plus they got the contract. If anything, we should move on to the next project," Chris says bravely. Opening my eyes, I lean my head back in my chair. It was a good idea to have some art placed up there, it really does calm me. I feel a rage build up within me, why do all these men think it's acceptable to question everything I do? Even before my father made me president, I didn't play that shit. So why is he trying me? I glare at Ron; he is looking at me waiting for instructions.

"Ron, why am I not talking to anyone in this room besides you right now?"

"Because we are scared little pussies who let some little trust fund crack baby out smart us by going behind our backs and getting a fresh money-making contract in London." I nod my head.

"Those were my words. Ron, why must everyone in this room refer to me as President and nothing else?"

"Because President, we are children that clearly forgot who you were while you were away, so you must now reintroduce yourself."

"So, if that is the fucking case Ron, why the fuck is everyone questioning me? There is no one in this room that can do my job. After costing me billions, you all sit here and have the audacity to ask questions? If I have to do everything myself, then what the fuck is the point of you people?" I stand, looking each person in the eye. Ron looks over at Matt.

"President, I'll have a name to you by the morning," Matt says while typing away on his phone.

"That's not good enough-," before Ron could finish saying exactly what I was thinking, I cut him off.

"I'm leaving for London tonight with the name of the person I need to see or every one of you will be out of a job. I had plans for that company, plans that would go over every one of your heads. If any of you used your brains for anything other than thinking of ways to undermine me, you would have seen the bigger picture." I sigh, forcing myself to calm down. "Gentlemen, this is your last chance. I'm sure the five of you can put your heads together and get me a name." With that, I walk out the conference room. I flew in from Mexico an hour ago. Ron was wise enough to wait until I landed to let me know what had happened. Immediately, I called for an emergency meeting. I have too much money invested to let Brook Co. acquire a win.

I think the meeting went well; the men have been put through worse. My father would have picked something up and had it flying across the room. I, on the other hand, am trying to stay calm.

Thankfully, I arrive home in time for dinner. I head straight to the dining room. As I get closer, I hear voices. The maids open the doors for me as I enter. The sight that greets me makes my blood boil. How could this day get any worse? It seems John, Justine and Samuel are joining us for dinner.

"The most beautiful girl in the world is back from her vacation," John stands, pulling my chair out for me. Taking my seat, I smile. I am happy to see him.

"It was work, not a vacation."

"Well sweetheart, anytime you can get away from this circus, you're on a vacation," he says, winking at me.

"John, let her sit down before you start with your nonsense," Shelly says smiling.

"Nonsense? I thought Ariah enjoyed me." He pouts playfully. Justine's laughter wipes the smile right off my face.

"I do, in fact, I like your company the most these days."

"What? What about me? And to think, I gave you my company, my life's work." My father's voice sounds slightly annoyed.

"Excuse me sir, you didn't just give me anything. You made me work for it. Plus, you are still the chairman."

"As long as you know," he says with a smug look on his face.

This is how dinner went, I pretended there are only four people at the table instead of six. Not too long ago, when I saw Samuel my heart couldn't stand it. I would have an episode or just cry. Now, I ignore him. I can finally be in the same room with him and his wife. After the wedding, Justine did not fuck with me again. It's nice to know she took my threat seriously. I will fuck Samuel if she ever tries me again.

I am a horrible person, but he is all I have known since I was 15. All my firsts are with him. Whenever I reminisce about something, he is there, helping me through it. I no longer lie to myself about being over him. I still love him very much. But I will not be a mistress, Samuel should have never given her that ring. He gave her power; he gave her everything. I'm becoming sad all over again, so I tune back into the conversation.

"There is a reason I've asked you all to come. Whether we like it or not, we're a family now." My father looks over to me. "Your aunt has been asking me for something that I cannot give her." He looks at Shelly. "Shells, I have decided that you should have a baby."

"What?" Shelly and I proclaim at the same time, my father continues.

"Not by me Shelly. I will not do it. John and I had a conversation about it, and we concluded that you should have a baby with John."

Everyone is quiet. I don't look to see everyone's expression because I cannot take my eyes off my father. I thought that he could no longer surprise me, but here I am, shocked by his announcement. This is fucked. Shelly is probably about to go bat shit crazy on him. How could he have a conversation with John about this first? I look over at John and he is eating casually as if this has nothing to do with him. If it wasn't official before, it is now, my family is fucked. As a matter of fact, we are all fucked.

"If that's what you want me to do," Shelly says hesitantly, staring at my father. And just like that, the three of them continue eating. I look over at Samuel who's looking at his father, then to Justine. She's wondering what the hell is going on. Samuel looks at me. He should speak up because I am not saying a thing. We are truly cowards.

Justine elbows Samuel. I roll my eyes, looking away. Tabitha walks over to me to let me know I have an urgent phone call. I know I shouldn't be doing work while having dinner, but this could be about London. I look over to my father, he nods his head in approval.

"Speak," I say in my most commanding voice.

"President, we've found out who Brad is signing the contracts with. It's a government worker named Mindy Strauss."

"Meet me at the airport in twenty minutes." I hang up and look at Shelly, she still has not lifted her head up from her plate. I should stay to figure this insanity out, but I know it will just be a waste of time. I do not have time to worry about these old people and their problems, I need to go get this company. "I'm sorry, you guys will have to excuse me."

"No problem, go take care of business. If you need us, we'll be right here. Make sure you get some sleep on the plane even if you have to force yourself, that time zone switch is no joke."

"Yes, daddy I know." I get up from the table to leave. It's a good thing I haven't unpacked my things from Mexico.

I direct the maids to bring those bags back down then I walk over to the car. "Ryan, this time I want you to travel with me. I feel uneasy with the new guy."

"You got it, Ariah," he says, closing the door as I step into the car.

Exhaustion blazes through my body as I head back to the hotel. The meeting with Mindy the bitch was not an easy endeavor. I am not sure if it was the time zone switch, the jet lag or her accent, but I'm completely drained. She's a smart woman, but in the end, she agreed to my terms. I had her sign the contract as we drank tea. What would have taken Brooke Co. weeks, took me hours. They should have just sold to me from the beginning. The only reason I want the shitty company is for some ports they own. I've decided to get into trading. If I am going to do that, I need ports for my ships, hence Brooke Co.

I could have told those shitheads at the office my plans, but I don't trust them. I do not trust anyone. It would only take one person to tell Brad, then he wouldn't sell, instead he would try to do business with me. Fuck that, I do not answer to anyone except daddy, oh and John, I guess I can't forget Shelly, but that's it. Looking out the window as we drive back to the hotel, I have a thought.

"Ron," he looks up, "do you drink, alcohol?"

"Yes ma'am, from time to time I have a drink."

"What drink will get me intoxicated quickly?"

"Well, that's hard to determine, what do you usually drink?"

"I don't, I only drink wine with dinner. But I want a hard liquor." Looking away I can tell he is taking me seriously; this is what I love about Ron.

"Whiskey, it's known to be very strong."

"Then whiskey it is. When we get to the hotel, I'm going to go have a drink at the bar."

After that, the car becomes quiet again, I am left to my thoughts. What was my father thinking? How is that a solution? Would he seriously be alright with Shelly and John sleeping together? Pulling up to the hotel, I step out the car and head straight to the bar. The place is empty, just the way I like it. I hate people. The bartender looks up at me, smiling.

"What can I get you?"

"Whiskey please," I say, taking a seat.

"Coming right up."

The bartender places the shot glass in front of me. I pick the glass up and swallow the entire contents. This shit is burning my chest as it goes down, I call the bartender over for another. After the fourth one, I can barely sit up straight. Leave it to Ron to tell me the truth. I see why my father would come home and have a drink; this numbing feels nice. I've always been expected to be perfect, hide my flaws, be ruthless, stay strong, rely on myself, stay one step ahead, never fail. But now, these things are taking a toll on me. I'm not allowed to show emotions, when I have so many. I was raised to be a successful woman in a man's world. The worst part of all this is that I have no one to take my mask off with. I am lonely. Will it always be like this? Will I never find someone I can lean on?

I can never let anyone know what I am thinking when I am thinking it, because they might use it against me. I can never show the damaged girl that I am. I must be the strong intelligent woman on the verge of being the most powerful woman in the world. The men who work under me hate me for being me, even though they cannot be better. No one can take my place; I know this fact and so do they. Those dumb bastards cannot outsmart anyone, not even themselves. It is lonely being at the top. I toss back another drink, getting drunk is much easier than I thought. I need to go to sleep, I am going home tomorrow. Attempting to stand, I almost lose my balance. I ease my body back into the seat just as someone takes a seat next to me. Looking at the stranger, I experience a strange sense of déjà vu.

"Dumpling," I quickly place my hand over my mouth. The beautiful specimen of a man looks at me, confused.

"I'm sorry, did you just call me food?" he asks, smirking.

Attempting to look normal, I give him a goofy smile. "Forgive me, you look like the man I'm dating in my head." The fuck, did I just say that shit out loud? That's it, no more drinking for me.

"The man in your head?" he asks, amused. "How about I get you a drink?" He waves the bartender over.

"No, thank you. I've had enough." I hiccup loudly. I need to go before I embarrass myself any further.

I look at the lovely stranger as he stares at me. He has a look in his eyes that I know all too well. One I haven't seen in a while. This man is looking at me like he wants to bend me over this bar, right here, right now. I take my bottom lip into my mouth biting it, then slowly releasing it. I watch as his eyes move from mine down to my lips. His smirk disappears as his left eye twitches. I feel my heart pumping at a ridiculously fast rate, I can feel my stomach tying into knots. This man wants to fuck me, and I am finding myself wanting to be fucked.

The alcohol is taking over, the words leave my lips before I can catch them.

"Do you want to fuck me?" The bartender looks at me as he places the drink on the counter. Narrowing his eyes, the handsome stranger chuckles.

"You have no idea the things I would like to do to you." He picks up his glass and brings it to his lips. "I don't like fucking women who are intoxicated." He tosses his drink back. I grab my purse off the stool next to me, where the fuck is my fucking phone. Digging at the bottom of my purse, I find it. Powering it back on, I dial Ron's number.

Holding the phone up to my ear, I do not take my eyes off him.

"Ms. Blackwood," Ron answers.

"Ron, how do I get sober within the next 30 minutes?"

I can hear him rummaging around, I must have woken him up. "Well, that depends, how much did you have to drink?"

"I had fou- no five shots of whiskey."

"Eat something with a lot of bread and grease like a burger or something. And drink lots of water. Can I go back to sleep now?"

"Yes, Ronny pooh, good night." I must really be fucked up. I never speak like this. I hang up the phone and call for the bartender. "Hey, let's give you a name. Can I call you Greg?" He looks around then nods his head yes. "Alright then, Greg, I need a burger, a big one and lots of water."

"Ma'am." Greg picks a phone up and begins speaking into it.

I look back at handsome, he has a grin on his face. He takes another swig of his drink. I reach over, taking the glass from him. "Hey, I don't want my partner to be drunk either."

"What do you suggest we do while we wait for you to sober up?"

"Talk! Hello handsome stranger, my name is Ariah Blackwood. I'm an extremely wealthy woman who fears nothing right now, there are 7 to 8 men here with guns aimed right at you." Handsome looks at me, putting his hand out.

"Hello gorgeous, I am Eugene Lee an extremely wealthy man that also has no fears." He moves closer to me. "Because there are 8 men with guns pointed at your 7 to 8 men who have guns pointed at me."

I take his hand, never mind what he just said to me. His face being so close has sent all my nerves into a frenzy. With my hand in his, I feel a shock go up my spine. Why am I acting like this over a stranger? Maybe because it's been a while since I've wanted someone sexually. This man's sex appeal, his whole aura has me intoxicated.

We are interrupted by food being placed in front of me. I devour the burger quickly. Eugene is watching me in fascination. I don't have time to worry about what I look like, I'm horny. For the first time in my life, I am going to have a one-night stand. I am getting excited just thinking about it. Damn, this burger is fucking good. Eugene is watching me eat so I lift my burger up, offering him a bite. Surprisingly, he takes a bite, I watch amazed as ketchup ends up on the corner of his mouth. He takes his finger and wipes the ketchup off, then puts his finger into his mouth. Fuck, I wish I were his finger.

"So, Ms. Ariah Blackwood, I take it you don't do this often?"

"What makes you say that?" I ask as I wipe my mouth with a napkin.

"Well, most women trying to seduce a man wouldn't swallow a whole burger the way you just did, not in front of said man anyway."

"Well, you said you wanted me sober, so I'm getting sober." Eugene becomes quiet as he watches me. He watches as I drink water, he watches as I unbutton my jacket making more room for the fries, he just watches. I feel myself becoming sober, and a bit embarrassed. I'm regretting sobering up; he must have read my mind.

"Are you sure you want to be fucked by me? I've been told I'm a bit cruel in the bedroom." His words awaken the competitive bitch in me.

"Cruel? I'm pretty sure I can do cruel." I grab my purse and stand. "Shall we, Mr. Lee?"

"Damn, I like the way you say that." Taking my hand, he leads the way.

Once we get to my room, my nerves kicks in. I have only been with one man. This is going to be the first time I am intimate with a stranger. I need to get my shit together; I want to do this. This man does not know me, and I do not know him. We will never see each other again.

"It's been a long day for me, I'm going to go shower. That is ok, right? I don't know the one-night stand protocol."

Taking his jacket off, he has a seat on the sofa. "That's fine."

I smile, skipping into the bathroom I tie my hair up. I do not need this shit frizzling up on me, I want to maintain the sexy chic look I have right now. I quickly clean myself, then jump out. I stare at myself in the mirror, what if he doesn't like my body? I scoff at the thought, I am motherfucking gorgeous. I brush my teeth, then I take the plush robe that's hanging on the door and wrap it around my body. I step out into the living room; Eugene stands to his feet.

"Do you need to shower? Did you also have a long day?" I ask nervously. What the fuck am I talking about right now?

"I showered before I went down to the bar. Any more questions?" he asks, smiling.

I shake my head. He takes his tie off, tossing it on the sofa. He starts to unbutton his shirt, but my body moves on its own, I stop his hands. I want to undress him; I want to take my time doing it. I look up at him as I push his shirt off his shoulders. The way he is looking down at me is making me have second thoughts. I feel like prey, I want to cower away and submit, but I refuse. I feel small shocks in my hands as they move down his smoothly shaped arms. I can tell my slow movements are frustrating him, but deep down I know that once we start, I'll lose control, he'll take over and that'll be all she wrote. Besides, I like the way his body feels under my hands. I unbuckle his pants, letting them fall to the floor.

Caressing my cheeks with both hands, he pushes my hair behind my shoulders. Eugene unties the string holding my robe together, his hands feel like silk as they gently push my robe off. I watch as he admires my body. I feel like a steak standing in front of a lion. Before I can say what I'm thinking, he grabs me by the back of my neck, kissing me.

His lips are soft against mine; he allows me to control the tempo of the kiss. I take my time, I want to feel everything. We begin walking backwards towards the bed, once I feel the bed on the back of my legs I am pushed down roughly. My heart is beating rapidly and I'm out of breath, but I refuse to lose focus. I look right at him as he looks down at me. His gaze is intense, I feel like I am about to be devoured by a beast. Eugene lets his underwear fall to the floor. Staring at his manhood, I gasp as he takes my foot into his mouth. There are no tender kisses, he is taking each toe into his mouth and biting down. Working his way up my leg to my thigh, the bites get harder, rougher.

Before I can utter a word of rebuke, I'm attacked. Taking my clit into his mouth, he begins sucking while using his tongue to beat it softly like a drum. I have never felt this sensation this quickly. I feel myself trying to get away from his mouth. I can't take it. I try to sit up, I feel like I'm going to explode. He sinks his fingers into my thighs and I know he is going to leave marks. I need to get away, his tongue is everywhere, the slurping sound from him leaving nothing behind is driving me crazy.

I feel myself about to release, yet he's not slowing down. Is he trying to kill me? I lift my waist, but he won't let me go. My whole body is shaking now, I can't stop it. My mouth is wide open, but no sound is coming out. I'm stuck in this moment of bliss; one I never want to be released from. Once he feels I've had enough he lets me go. If I had the energy, I would get up and run because he still has that hungry look in his eyes. Taking my legs, he closes them, then pushes my knees to my chest. He takes my arms, wrapping them around my legs.

"Hold these," he demands as if these are not my legs but objects that need to be held in place. I do as I'm told though. I stare at him, I feel like a little bunny and he is a big bad wolf. I do not like feeling like this for many reasons.

"I won't hurt you, if you want me to back off, I will," he looks at the position he has me in. "It'll be hard, but I will." I take a deep breath; I feel so small. Taking his dick into his hand, he begins rubbing against my entrance. His teasing is driving me crazy; I close my eyes, waiting in anticipation.

I open my eyes as he places his dick at my opening, ramming into me. Pulling all the way out, he pushes all the way back in. He's driving my body crazy; all my muscles are tensing up. I'm trying to hold on to the feeling he gives me, then easily takes away. He finds his rhythm, pulling all the way out just to ram back in. I'm holding on to my legs with both arms for dear life. He smacks my thighs every now and then. My feet are hitting his chest, I hope I leave a bruise.

Eugene begins thrusting in and out of me so fast and so hard that I know I am going to ache in the morning. Usually when I have sex I have to concentrate, focus on finding that good feeling, right now it keeps sneaking up on me. I am trying to not give in so quickly, but he's not giving me a choice. I feel myself trying to get away again, he smiles down at me. Turning my body to the side, he holds me down with one hand on my waist, the other on my thigh.

This position changes nothing, I continue feeling unbearable bliss. I need a break, I need to catch my breath. I feel like he's trying to fuck me to death, I can't take this. I try to get away again, by straightening out my legs, just to give myself a little relief, him continuously hitting my spot is driving me insane, it is becoming painful. This time he growls, flipping me on my stomach, he positions me on my knees. He forces my arms behind my back, then bends down to my ear.

"Let's see you get away now." What have I done to myself? I may not be able to walk in the morning.

Waking up, I stare at the ceiling. I sit up on my elbows, looking around the room. It looks like a tornado ran through it. I passed out last night. I have never passed out during sex before. I try sitting up, but just as I thought, everything hurts. I wobble my way into the bathroom, I look in the mirror and see bite marks everywhere. I feel and look like I've been in a fight, but I have this dumb ass smile on my face. I am never having a one-night stand again.

I have to catch a flight back to the States in one hour. I step into the shower, cleaning myself as quickly as I can. If I ever see Dump- Eugene again, I'm going to slap him, then probably kiss him. I smile at the thought, stepping out the bathroom I begin getting dressed. Hearing a knock at the door, I assume it's Ron. I walk out the bathroom as best as I can. Ron has all my things packed and is staring at me with a judgmental face.

"What? Doesn't everyone get at least one casual hook up in their lifetime?"

"Sure, everyone does, but you don't."

"Well, I do now." I put my sunglasses on, attempting to look graceful. I gracelessly wobble out the door. When we get down to the hotel lobby, I look out the door, the paparazzi is everywhere. I close my jacket as best as I can. I do not need to be photographed with bite marks on my neck. I look over to Ryan. "I can't fake it past all that, my legs hurt."

Smiling, he quickly swoops me into his arms. As we walk past the paparazzi, I smile and wave as they ask questions I refuse to answer. We get to the car and Ryan sets me down gently.

"Thank you." He closes my door and I sit back enjoying the ride.

Chapter Seventeen

"I have something to say," my father says sternly. The dinner chatter stops, with my fork still in my hand, I look around our table. Shelly is looking at me, while everyone else has their eyes on my father. I raise my eyebrows at her, silently asking if she knows what kind of bomb will be dropped on us this evening. The last dinner announcement made us all question my father's sanity. However, looking at Shelly's protruding belly, I would say they are all truly insane. I always wondered how Samuel and I survived high school. But the real question is, how the fuck did we survive our families? I decide to focus on my food. I am sure my father is about to say something asinine, however, I'm starving.

"Ariah, this pertains to you, so please listen." Setting my fork down, I take my napkin, wipe my mouth and give him my undivided attention. "As we all knew you would, you have successfully taken over the company." I smile.

"You are everything I raised you to be. Sure, I've given you all the tools you needed to be successful, but the way you have used them... let's just say you, my wonderful daughter, have exceeded my expectations in every way possible." I feel my eyes about to water. I have worked my entire life to please this man and make him proud; to be his heir, to never have him wish for one second that I was born a man.

"Unlike myself, I wish to ensure that you have people around you who are helpful, that can assist you in any way possible. I am a man that could have anything in the world, anything." He takes Shelly's hand. "Except time. I cannot live forever, Ariah. I will not be around forever to ensure that you are untouchable. Right now, you can fly as high as you want and go as low as you can, but when John and I are gone, who will you have?"

"Father, what are you talking about? Are you dying? Why are you talking like you're about to leave me?" My heart feels like it's about to explode in my chest. The room feels like it's spinning and I clench my stomach to keep the vomit from spewing out.

John grabs my hand, "Ariah calm down, deep breaths, take a deep breath."

I look at John, "what's going on?"

"You're getting married." Staring at John, I drown everything else out. I heard exactly what he said, but my mind needs a bit more time to register his words. Turning to face my father, I feel my anger rising.

"Excuse me?"

"Like Samuel and Justine here, you will be married." I glare at him.

"Yes father, I know what it means to get married, however I don't understand what you mean when you say that I'll be getting married."

"You and your fiancé are to be married." He appears unmoved by my tone.

"Fiancé?" I ask, baffled.

"Ariah, come on. Why do you think John and I were so against you and Samuel? Even before the both of you were born, you were promised to someone else." I look at Samuel as he glares at John. My father begins eating his food. "Justine's mother is a college friend of ours-."

"Daddy, I don't care about your college friend. I need to know why I have a fiancé that I've never met or heard of. Shelly, did you know about this?" I look at her as she sighs.

"Fucking great, another secret that the two of you have been keeping from me. Is there anything else? Please don't wait until years from now to let me know."

"Sweetheart, how do you think two college kids were able to become successful so quickly? Your father's and my success would have happened regardless, but without a little help we'd still be building." John looks at Samuel. "Legacy, the most important thing to us is our legacy. The shit we leave behind when we die, and that shit is the two of you."

My father chimes in. "Fucking right. Samuel, your grandfather left your father many things, but stability was not one of them. Ariah, you know where we came from, that shit is tragic. The two of you can hate us for not allowing your relationship, but that shit was doomed from the start."

"Why couldn't that be our choice?" Samuel asks, speaking up for the first time. I look across the table at Samuel in amazement. This is the first time I have ever heard him speak back to our parents.

"You guys were unlucky," John says, tossing back his drink.

Placing his knife and fork on the table my father looks at me. "We decided that we would keep our success in house, no outsiders. John, Claire, Yoo Joon and I made a promise to one another."

"Yoo Joon?" I say, thoroughly confused.

"Yes, all of us have remained at the top in our respective fields because we helped each other in the beginning. Ariah, it's a lonely world out there; allies are needed to navigate through it. So, we promised that our children would marry each other in the future." He continues eating as if he hadn't just dropped a huge bomb.

"Justin, Claire's son, is a fucking idiot." I look at John, still unable to believe this is happening. "So, she's giving everything to Justine. Justin doesn't feel Justine should have her mother's company. In order to protect her daughter and her own assets, she is providing her daughter with protection." John looks at Samuel. "A protection that was promised to her before she was born. With me and Samuel by her side, Justine is now untouchable and Samuel has a strong ally, like a sword ready to slay anyone in its way." I look down at my plate shaking my head. My father slams his fist on the table.

"We have done what we must to protect all of you. Be grateful, things could have been a lot fucking worse. I am tired of explaining myself to you." He looks around the table. "The three of you have life at its fucking throat. We did that, everything you can dream of you can make a reality. You're welcome."

Listening to everything is making my mind go into overdrive. What the fuck, be grateful? As if we didn't sacrifice and work hard to earn the shit they have given us. John is right, this is a goddamn circus and my father is the ringmaster. Everything about my life has been planned out to a tee. When will I be able to make my own decisions? While deep in thought, I faintly hear Shelly calling my name.

"Ariah, Ariah are you alright?"

"No, Shelly I am not." I look at my father. "What is there for me to decide for myself? You have my whole life planned out. I will not marry a stranger. I have never once gone against you, but this I will not do." I stand and walk out the dining room.

"We leave tomorrow morning. If I have to have Ryan drag your ass out that room like a 3-year-old, then so be it," my father shouts after me. I am not going any goddamn where.

How is this my fucking life? Am I not a grown ass woman? I am the president of one of the biggest companies in the world. I have control over billions of dollars. My name speaks volumes in boardrooms across the planet, so could someone explain to me why the fuck am I being tossed over Ryan's shoulder like a 3-year-old? As Ryan walks up the stairs of one of my father's planes, I start punching him in the back. This is so frustrating; Ryan sits me down in a chair across from my father.

"I said I wasn't going," I say through clenched teeth.

"Yes, I heard." My father lights a cigar. "Ariah, why would you wait until your twenties to rebel? You had all those teenage years to get all this out." I think I hate my father; he sits there with a smug look on his face as he puffs his cigar. I sit back, fold my arms and look out the window. The pilot announces that we are about to take off and to buckle up. I don't move, I don't want to go anyway. My father begins laughing. Standing, he walks over and buckles my seat belt.

"Why are you being a baby about this, Ariah?"

"I'm not being a baby." I start kicking my feet. "Daddy, I don't want to marry a stranger." Once the plane is in the air, the pilot announces we can take our seat belts off. My father comes to sit next to me, I place my head on his shoulder.

"How have things been at the office?" he asks, holding my hand.

"The same as always, stupid people trying to be smart. Smart people pretending to be dumb, they are all snakes."

"Exactly, they all want what's yours. They have nothing of their own, so they want what's yours. That is the world, people will look at you and underestimate you. They will think that you can't handle shit. They will think that they can take care of your shit better than you. You know that's not true. You can hold your own against anybody in the world and win. But while you fight that war, who will have your back?" I sit quietly, listening.

"Use this marriage, use it to protect yourself. If you want to love, then do that, I don't care. You and everything I am giving you are my legacy. I am giving you the world, use that shit however you want. You know me, once I give you something, it's yours. This marriage is just another safety net, not just for you, but for him too." He wraps his arm around me. "Just think, with this marriage, he doesn't have to fight against you, but with you. The two of you coming together will give you unimaginable power." He kisses my forehead. "Get some rest, it's going to be a long flight."

Feeling my father move his arm from around my head wakes me up.

"Good, you're awake, go take a shower and get dressed. I'm sure you don't want to meet your future husband," he waves his hand in my direction, "looking like that." I look down at myself, I'm still in my pajamas.

"Whose fault is it that I look like this? You had Ryan throw me over his shoulder at the crack of dawn."

"I told you we were leaving, be sure to brush your teeth too."

"Daddy," I put my hand up to my mouth, then blow in it. I quickly head to the room at the back of the plane. I have clothes hanging on the rack and all my things are in the bathroom, my father came prepared. Once I've showered, I brush my teeth and get dressed. When I go out to sit with my father, I notice he has changed as well. I plop down next to him. The pilot announces that we are getting ready to land and to put our seat belts on.

"Daddy, where are we?"

He's busy scrolling through his tablet. What kind of business is he taking care of?

"South Korea." I nod my head.

"What have you been doing on your tablet this whole time?"

"Shopping. I'm getting the nursery together for the baby. John thinks his will be better. That motherfucka wouldn't know taste if it was licking his balls." I roll my eyes; how can they still be petty old men given the situation? I sit back, put my seat belt on and relax as we land.

I have never been to South Korea before. I look like a tourist looking out my window with my mouth wide open. I always turn into a kid around Charles Blackwood. We pull up to a restaurant, Ryan opens my door and I step out. I wait for my father to walk around the car then I wrap my arm around his. Like a switch, all the nervous jitters in me are hidden by my confident stride and piercing eyes. We walk up to the hostess, but before we can get any words out, the hostess speaks first.

"Please allow us to take your coats, then if you will follow me, Mr. Lee is waiting for you." I follow behind my father; eyes watch as we walk by. Have they never seen black people before? Maybe they think we're celebrities. We arrive at a room in the back of the restaurant, my father walks in first.

"Joon, I love the way you fucking do things, you smooth mothafucka." He walks over to his old friend, pulling him in for a hug.

"Charles, I see you still talk like a sleazy drug dealer."

I want to be polite and introduce myself, but I can't speak. My feet are stuck in place, I can't fucking move. I want to run away from his gaze, I watch as his eyes move up and down my body undressing me, forcing me to remember that night. A night that was meant to happen once, with a person I would never meet again. I can hear my heart thumping loudly in my chest. Why is Eugene Lee standing next to my father?

"This, Joon, is my greatest creation," my father says, looking at me. Snapping out of my trance, I walk over to shake the older man's hand.

"Hello, I'm Ariah Blackwood," I say smiling.

"I am Lee Yoo Joon and this," he looks over to Eugene, "is my son, Lee Yoo Jin." Avoiding eye contact with whomever this is standing in front of me, I look at the table and notice there are only two seats. I look at my father with questioning eyes. What is he up to?

"Ah, me and Joonie are going to go catch up. You and your future husband should get to know each other." With that, the old bastards walk out the room laughing. I look at the table and take a seat, Yoo Jin does the same. We stare at each other, neither of us speaking. Did this bastard give me a fake name?

"Hello stranger?" I grit out through clenched teeth. He ignores my anger.

"Lee Yoo Jin is my Korean name. I went to school in the states, the kids there pronounced it as Eugene. In America, I am Eugene Lee." My one-night stand was a setup. Has there ever been a coincidence in my life?

"How long have you known about me?" I ask. Why am I always last to the party?

"Two years. When my father told me about the arrangement he had with Charles, I was livid. I flew to America immediately to break it off with you, but when I found you," he pauses, picking up his wine glass, "you were on a park bench crying. It looked like you were already having a bad day."

Breaking eye contact, I look down at my hands. As always, everything happens to me in a fucked-up way. I never get enough time to be mad at one thing, because something else always happens. I am waiting for someone to jump out with a camera and tell me this has all been one big joke.

"So why not break it off now?" I ask, avoiding his eyes.

"You know why."

"No, I do not. Enlighten me."

"You are Ariah Blackwood, and I am Lee Yoo Jin, this is big business, among other things." He takes a sip of his wine.

"Other things?" I ask with raised eyebrows. This time he doesn't reply. His begins looking at his glass as he swirls the liquid around. He takes his bottom lip into his mouth while smiling. Oh goodness, is that a dimple? Our eyes lock and memories from the night we shared charge at me. I look away before I lose all common sense.

"There are other rich women for you to do big business with." I say, trying to keep the conversation on track.

"I want you."

"You want me?" I ask, doubting his words.

"I want you," he says again, throwing me off. Why is he so straightforward? I'm not use to this. I laugh trying to play off his intensity.

"What? Do you love me or something?"

"I like you," he pauses, "a lot."

The mood becomes serious again. I look around awkwardly, I don't know how to respond. If this were a battle I would be losing. This man has seen me naked, yet I sit before him unable to shake off this shyness.

"So, we're getting married?" I ask, deciding to get serious as well.

"Yes."

"Is there a woman I should know about? A high school sweetheart, a first love?" The question got away from me before I could catch it.

"No, Ariah." I could melt at hearing him say my name. "There are no other women. For the past two years, there has been just one woman, you." I take a deep breath. I need to calm myself. Why is my body reacting to him? Why is he staring at me so intensely?

"We just met, and you don't know me." I hear the crack in my voice. I need to get my emotions under control.

"Ariah," there he goes again. "I know everything there is to know about you." His stare is slowly weighing me down.

"What do you think you know, Yoo Jin?" I wanted to hear myself say his name.

A smirk appears on his face. I begin fidgeting in my seat as he leans forward, looking straight into my eyes.

"I know all the good things and all the bad things," he says holding my gaze.

Eugene sits back in his chair, placing one of his legs over the other. Why does he look at me like that? I believe the words he says. That alone lets me know I need to get out of here. I smack my lips, standing to leave. Before I can get to the door, I am pinned up against a wall. I feel his lips brush against mine as I look at him in disbelief.

"Leaving so soon, Mrs. Lee?"

This is too much, why am I so taken with this man? The pure lust I'm feeling is exhilarating. My will is caving and there's nothing to stop it. I've only felt this way one other time in my life. And because of it, I told a stranger my deepest darkest secrets. I said I would never do this again. Eugene has me on the verge of a free fall.

"I can't breathe," I say honestly.

"Why?" he asks amused.

"You are too close, it's intoxicating." I squeeze my thighs together. If I could pinch myself, I would.

"Is that all you're running away from?" he asks knowingly.

"You don't know me," I answer defiantly.

Gently kissing my lips, he whispers, "I know you Ariah Blackwood, I know you very well. This mask you're hiding behind is so well crafted that the people around you don't even know the real you." He kisses my cheek. "They don't know just how fragile you truly are." His warm lips drift to my neck. "But I do, I know that with just a little push I can have all of you. Don't worry, you'll never be taken for granted in my care." He stares into my eyes as his nose touches mine. "I know that you can't wait to give yourself away."

I feel my eyes water, as his words replay in my head. Why can he see through me? I just built myself back up, I can't fall again. My father is wrong, I don't need him. I don't need protecting. I can protect myself. All I need is me. Why the fuck am I about to cry? Fuck! I need to get away from him, far away. I'm doing my best to keep my mouth closed, because I know I will say something stupid.

This man has been in my head ever since I left the park that day. I used his image to distract me from the sadness I almost let consume me. Besides Samuel, I'd never been attracted to another man. Yet here I am, drooling. My body wants to be taken by Eugene, while my heart is screaming no. This is not a one-night stand, this would be a marriage.

Closing my eyes, I take a deep breath. I feel hot, vulnerable, aroused. All my senses are on full alert because of this man. I can't believe after everything, I'm still this fucking dumb. Eugene looks at me as if daring me to ask, he knows what I want to say.

"You think you can handle all of me? Everything I have to offer?" I ask through trembling lips. My heartbeat slows as I wait in anticipation for his answer.

"I know I can, all you have to do is fall, I'll catch you." I feel my knees buckle, but before I fall, he grabs me. "Where are you going?"

"You told me to fall." I am once again letting someone in, why do I do this to myself? A lone tear falls down my face. Wiping the tear away, Eugene begins kissing me and I kiss him back with all my heart.

To Be Continued!

Before You Go

Deep Breaths: Inhale is book one in this series of three. Deep Breaths: Suffocation is book two and will be coming soon. In the meantime, feel free to check out my other works. You can easily access them by using the QR code below.

Also be sure to follow me @RichandaBynum on my socials to keep up with projects I'm working on next. I will be back soon.

Thank you for reading my work!

www.ingramcontent.com/pod-product-compliance
Lightning Source LLC
Chambersburg PA
CBHW020535020726
47494CB00006B/1783